The Gathering at Hope

Terry M. Beard

ISBN: 978-1-7333102-4-6 paperback

ISBN: 978-1-7333102-5-3 ebook

Hope Series Book 3 First Edition

Christian Romance

Prepared for publication by 40DayPublishing.com

Cover design by www.40DayGraphics.com

Printed in the United States of America

Acknowledgements

I love you, Lord. You are my everything. Thank You for guiding me through the entire process of writing, *The Gathering at Hope.*

My family and friends have encouraged me each step of the way. I appreciate and love y'all more than you know.

The Writers Group of Greater San Antonio read and re-read my pages. Their critiquing expertise and helpful suggestions made this book come to fruition. Thank you!

The experts at 40 Day Publishing motivated me to keep writing and creating. Their professional suggestions guided me throughout this journey. I am thankful they published another book in the Hope Series.

Doris Jo Lewis edited *Inn at Hope* and I am thankful she edited this book, too. She is proficient in her field and notices even the smallest detail. More importantly, she is a true friend and wonderful reflection of Jesus.

Carol Holland has been my Beta Reader for all three books in the Hope Series. Her ability to critique a story from beginning to end is amazing. She is a long-time friend and true witness for our Lord.

Suzann F. Mohacsi, Ph.D., perused the back of the book blurb for each of the books in this series. She read and suggested ideas masterfully. We've known each other for years and are related because of Jesus.

Thank you, Barry, for helping me with all the technical things that overwhelm me! You've come to the rescue more times than I can count.

Dedication

To my family, which included our Great Dane, Trixie. She graced our home for fourteen and a half years. We are so thankful!

Chapter 1

Torrential rain and high humidity inundated the Piedmont area. Flash flood warnings splashed across television screens and blasted on the radio. The Reedy River swelled over its banks and Huff Creek, a branch off the Saluda River, flooded area roads. Unbearably warm temperatures smothered the tiny town of Hope, South Carolina. Ducks in the lake across from Beaufort Street reveled in the water as rain pelted their living quarters. The nearby gazebo was empty. No chairs lined either side of a make-shift center aisle. No outdoor ceremony. Today of all days--my dear friend, Lauren's, wedding day.

**

I parked my car in a spot on the main street. When I slipped out of the front seat of my VW Bug, my orange plastic poncho blew in the wind. My goal: Sweets from Bitty's Buns. The French door to the bakery stuck from the humidity then popped open with force. I barreled inside and fell smack dab into my long-time friend, Lauren.

"Rae, what are you doing here? You might slip or something!"

"What are you doing here? You're supposed to be eating breakfast with your folks at the Inn." I slid the hood off my long frizzy hair. "Plus, we're supposed to meet at the Inn in a couple hours to get ready for your wedding. Have you forgotten?" I pretended to scowl.

Lauren snatched several napkins off the counter and attempted to dry her black/white striped rain jacket. "Mom and Dad are eating at the Inn with all the family who've come into town." She paused, "I thought you were in the kitchen helping Chef Molly. I just couldn't sit and chat with everyone. I needed some time to breathe." She took an exaggerated deep breath. "I'm feeling overwhelmed." Lauren wadded the wet napkins and shoved them into her jacket pocket. "Didn't you get my text?"

Before I could answer, Natalie, the owner of the bakery, fluttered from behind the counter. "Rae Long Byer, you need to dry off before you and that baby you're incubating catch a cold. What are you doing out in this monsoon?" She didn't wait for my response, but instead gently pressed Lauren aside and wiped off my drippy plastic covering with a paper towel. "Let's get you out of this contraption." She pulled and prodded then finally slipped the trash bag sized rain poncho over my head. "Ah, now that's better. Sit down, dear, and put up your feet. Let me get you some decaf tea." Natalie pointed to a small table for two at the front of the bakery. "Sit there, girls. Lauren, happy wedding day. Are you getting cold feet, honey? Don't worry. It's normal. Now sit down and I'll get you whatever your heart desires." She smoothed back a wisp of her salt-and-pepper hair.

Lauren and I followed her orders and sat.

I slid out of my plastic sandals. "Natalie, I'm here to get the cinnamon buns for the guests at the Inn."

"You just missed Joe. Didn't your husband tell you he picked up everything? He wanted to save you a trip." She drummed her fingers on the back of my chair, shook her head, and scampered to the counter. "I'll get your tea. How about a scone? Lauren? Coffee and a scone, dear?"

Lauren and I nodded, then I slid my phone from my pocket and noticed an earlier text from Joe saying he was getting goodies from Bitty's. He wanted to make sure I didn't get out in this deluge. The second message was from my dear, dear friend.

I reached across the table and took Lauren's hand. "I'm so sorry I didn't see your message. Here I am, your matron of honor, and I'm shirking my duties. Can you forgive me?"

Lauren's eyes misted. "There's nothing to forgive, Sis. Look how God kind of answered my text. He put you at Bitty's Buns the same time as I'm here. I love how that worked out."

My phone buzzed.

Joe. "Wife, are you okay?"

"I didn't see your text, Husband. I'm at Bitty's Buns with Lauren."

His laughter filled the phone. "Can't believe our paths didn't cross since we live in the same place. Tell Lauren I said, hi." He added, "Wait a minute, is the wedding still on?"

I whispered. "Yes, it's still a go."

"Beautiful, I already picked up the cinnamon buns. Love you."

"Love you, too."

I slid my phone back inside my purse.

Lauren pulled off her rain boots and slid them under her chair. "My feet are swelling. What if I don't fit into my wedding shoes tonight?" She stuffed her umbrella between her chair and the window ledge. "That doggone red dirt is going to get on my wedding dress and ruin everything. I'm stressing." She blew her nose loudly then rubbed her temples. "I can't believe its raining. I know the ceremony will be fine at Fenster Haus, but I wanted it outside. This doesn't fit into my plan, Sis."

Natalie discreetly slid our orders in front of us, stepped back, then folded her arms in front of her. "Lauren, sorry for eavesdropping. Dear girl, I'll bet moving to Hope, South Carolina, from Maryland was never in your plan. And look at you now. Getting married to a fine young man who you'd never have met if you hadn't followed God's lead. You've tackled so much more than a few raindrops. Your wedding will be wonderful despite the weather. God has good adventures lined up for you and Mick. I just know it." She gently squeezed Lauren's shoulder. "Okay, gals, I'm off my soapbox." She moved to the back of the tiny dining area and refilled coffee cups for guests at other tables.

Lauren slid her chair back, walked in her sock feet to the back of the bakery, leaned down, and hugged Natalie's tiny frame. I bit my lower lip to squelch a giggle.

When Lauren returned to our table, I pulled the phone from my purse. We perused the detailed list for today's wedding day plans as we finished our light breakfast. A busy day ahead. No worries. Or so we thought.

* * *

Power outage. No air-conditioning. No plug-in phone chargers. No lights. No wedding. The news circulated throughout the town until my mother-in-law, Grace, also known as the President of the Historical Society, put a squelch on it. Anyone who had an ounce of energy left on their phone received her all-important e-mail:

The Veterinary Hospital has a humongous generator at the barn. Our fabulous vet, Val, said she's willing to host the wedding ceremony. Might be a little unorthodox. Lauren and Mick shuddered at the thought, until they realized they'd have to wait to marry if they didn't take the option. So, ceremony is at original time. BTW bring candles. The couple likes the idea of a candlelight ceremony in the barn.

Joe and I laughed hysterically at the e-mail from Grace Byer. Everyone in town already knew the change of plans before she sent her official manuscript with detailed instructions. The wedding party readied for the event in the barn. Or the official title for this evening: the ceremonial wedding site.

* * *

The left side of the wooden barn housed sheep. A blanket filled with orange tabby kittens and their momma nestled nearby. Horses on the mend sheltered in stalls on the right side. The soft sounds of the animals made the atmosphere feel rather ethereal.

Val nixed the idea of candles unless they were battery operated. No fire. The string quartet from Greenville canceled due to flooding in our area. Lottie, the Historical Society secretary, volunteered to play the wedding march on her portable keyboard. The pastor was in Anderson, S.C. The weather held him there, but Joe found a substitute.

Lauren looked breathtaking in her lace mermaid style gown. She flowed down the makeshift aisle with her daddy on her arm. Mick, her soon-to-be husband, waited eagerly.

I stood next to my dear friend and Joe stood next to Mick. Quinn, our Texas cowboy uncle, officiated the ceremony.

* * *

After the ceremony, Lauren shuffled through the straw laden barn floor to my side. "Rae, wasn't this the craziest wedding you've ever been to?" She squeezed me tightly. "But Mick and I loved it."

"Sis, it was the best. Who would've ever thought you'd marry in a barn, wearing sneakers, with a Texas Rancher officiating the ceremony?" I adjusted the spaghetti strap on my tea length dress. "By the way, you are glamorous and breathtaking, Lauren." I pulled a piece of straw from the messy braided bun at the nape of her neck.

"Straw in my hair? You've got to be kidding me." She laughed. "By the way, Sis, thanks for letting us stay in a cottage. We'll head on our honeymoon as soon as the weather lets up and flights resume." She beamed.

"Your luggage is already at the cottage, courtesy of Uncle Quinn and Joe." I hugged her waist. "I'm so glad our lives didn't turn out like we dreamed. Just think of all the adventures we'd have missed!" I pulled my orange poncho off a nearby hook. "Here Sis. It's raining cats and dogs. Slip this over your gown. I also brought your rain boots." I patted a wooden bench. "Sit here and put everything on, please." I glanced over my shoulder and saw Joe and Mick cackle with laughter. "Mick, you'd better stop laughing."

Joe held a large orange poncho. "Here you go, Mick. Might as well put it on. You and Lauren are a team now."

Uncle Quinn bellowed. "Hey, Mick, you don't need rain boots you need cowboy boots. City slicker."

The newlyweds cautiously stepped around the fenced area, which secured newborn sheep and their mommas. The guests lined either side of the huge barn doors. They clinched umbrellas to no avail, cheered, and hugged the poncho clad newlyweds as they tromped through the sliding doors at the back of the huge facility. Lauren and Mick slipped into a waiting limo and headed to the Inn at Hope. They didn't know Joe had turned on the fireplace and placed the ***Do Not Disturb*** sign on the cottage door when he delivered the luggage earlier.

* * *

As Joe and I left the ceremony, we jostled along in his old Ford truck. He pulled over periodically and wiped the windshield with an old cloth, since the window defroster had died. We dodged potholes on the winding road and stopped as rain blocked our view. We didn't mind. The extra time was filled with extra kisses. Blush.

* * *

Power returned shortly after we arrived home at the Inn. Joe's rain boots came in handy as he stomped and tromped through the globs of clay to deliver goodie baskets filled with sparkling cider, assorted cheeses, and crackers to each cottage. I'd offered to help carry an umbrella to shield him from the rain, but he declined. The **Do Not Disturb** sign at Mick and Lauren's cottage, swung in the wind maybe as a reminder to stay away. No need to deliver one single item to the honeymooners. Joe and I stocked up their refrigerator with all kinds of goodies before the wedding. Of course, the two of them had each other. Nothing more needed.

* * *

Warm bath, powder blue cotton gown, tootsies under the duvet. Sleeping hubby. Snoring canines. I patted my tummy. Thank You for these little ones. Good night, Lord.

And now these three remain: faith, hope and
love. But the greatest of these is love.
1 Corinthians 13:13

Chapter 2

I awoke to the sound of rain pelting the upstairs window. Joe left me a note on one of our fluffy pillows. *Beautiful, forgot about meeting at school. I better not forget next week when I start Dad's job. Dogs fed. Love you.* I smooched his note, placed it on the side table, shuffled out of bed, and readied for the day. I giggled at the sight of my three-month babies bump and dressed into a loose-fitting, pink polka-dot top, stretchy jeans, and gardening boots. My brush chugged through my long, thick mane to no avail. The pink clip in my frizzy hair couldn't tame the curls. Not one little iota.

Lauren and Mick remained in their cottage for two days. The **DO NOT DISTURB** sign still clung to their doorknob.

It shocked me to see a text from her.

Lauren: We're flying to WY. Mick's gma passed away this a.m.

Me: Oh, no!

Lauren: Mick's the executor. Please pray.

Me: I will, Sis

Texting stopped and my phone buzzed. Lauren.

"Rae, I feel horrible about Grandma Treavor's passing. Mick and his grandma were so close." She sniffled.

"How can Joe and I help?"

"You're helping with Heidi dog, and we're so thankful. Mick reserved a spot in long-term parking at the airport so that's taken care of."

"Is Mick at the cottage?" I squinted through the raindrops on the bedroom window and noticed the sport's car was gone.

"He's with his parents and going through paperwork and stuff. I'll join them in a bit. We have flight reservations for tonight, Sis."

"Lauren, be honest, do you mind if I trot over to your bungalow?"

"I'd love that."

I traipsed down the back stairs, "Good morning, Miss Molly. Thanks for weathering this storm and coming in today." I giggled at the sight of the four mammoth hounds standing watch in the kitchen. I'm sure they hoped Molly would spill a few fried potatoes and scrambled eggs, and they'd gladly help with cleanup.

"Duty calls, dear. Glad I got here without having to swim. Come to think of it, I can't even tread water." She grimaced. "All the guests called in their order for take-out breakfasts this morning. Kramer and his brother, Nathaniel, are delivering to the cottages."

"I could have done it, Molly."

"I made an executive decision. You're pregnant and these young men want to help." She inched closer to where I stood. "Plus, Kramer loves seeing the dogs." She whispered. "He also knows Kelly will be here in a few. She's helping me place everything in boxes."

"You spoil me, Molly. I hope I'm half the mother you are." I snatched an umbrella from the bucket near the back door. "It's gonna sound silly, but I've been contemplating baby's names. It dawned on me when I first met Kelly, you called her Mandy?" I shrugged.

"Oh, Rae." She laughed. "Mandy is her first name and Kelly is her middle name. It's not uncommon in the south to use the middle name."

"Well, that explains it then." I twittered.

She hugged my frame. "By the way, where are you off to in this weather?"

"Girl-talk with Lauren."

"I understand. Be extra careful." She pivoted and dolloped butter onto individual brioche rolls.

*　*　*

I plowed through the watery parking area until my boot got stuck in the red clay. I twisted and turned till the doggone thing unstuck. With my umbrella teetering in one hand, I trudged on and arrived at cottage four. Lauren and Mick's place.

My dear sister and I chattered non-stop. I cozied into the chair near the fireplace while Lauren packed her suitcase. "What's Mick's grandma's name? Do you mind if I let the Historical Society ladies know?"

"I don't mind at all. Her name is Alana G. Treavor. She's my dad-in-law's mother. She turned her home into a bed and breakfast when she was a young woman." Lauren giggled. "Sound a little familiar, Miss Inn at Hope owner?" She attempted to close her luggage. "Rae, come here and sit on this thing. Your extra weight..." She stopped mid-sentence.

I pushed out of the chair and pointed at her suitcase. "Put it on the floor. These babies and I'll give it the best we've got." Chuckle.

She followed my command and the luggage closed and locked easily with my assistance.

"See, Sis, my babies are already lending a helping hand." I patted my tummy.

"You crazy girl. I love those little ones." A knock on the door startled us. "Wonder who that could be?" She opened it and there stood Kramer with two boxed breakfasts.

"Hi, Mrs. Treavor. Your breakfast is served. I hope you and Mr. Treavor enjoy." He noticed me standing near the fireplace. "Hi, Mrs. Byer. Did you want breakfast, too?"

"No, Kramer. I'm good. Thanks for delivering the meals."

"You're welcome."

Lauren closed the door and placed both boxes on the round table near the French doors. "I didn't know Kramer was working for you now. I'm impressed that you've expanded your staff." She smiled.

"Molly asked him and his brother, Nathaniel, to help."

"Ah, that was nice of her."

"Plus, her daughter, Kelly, will be lending a helping hand, too."

"Now I get the picture." She grinned.

"Well Sis, I'll get going. I'm only a text or call away if you need anything. I love you." I hugged her waist tightly. "I'll miss you, Lauren."

"I already miss you. I love you, too."

The torrential rain had turned into a drizzle. I held onto my umbrella with both hands and splashed through a few puddles toward home.

* * *

Puffs, Buddy, Trixie, and Heidi greeted me at the back door. I dropped my umbrella in the mud room and slid out of my boots. "Come here, you sweet things." I kissed each noggin and schlepped into the kitchen in my stocking feet.

Chef Molly pulled a freshly made tray of scones from the oven. "Now sit down, dear. How about some decaf tea? You need to warm up." She slid a pecan scone onto a plate next to eggs and bacon. "Protein is a must."

I hugged my dear friend. "Molly, you're the best. Thank you for pampering us." I patted my tummy and slid onto a stool.

She winked. "I know a little something about babies, dear one. And you have more than one in that precious baby bump of yours."

Before we shared another word, the back door blew open and in flew my mother-in-law, Grace. She wiped her boots on the rug, flung her plastic rain cap into the mud room sink, and stormed into the kitchen. She had a bee in her bonnet, as the expression goes. And I didn't want to get stung. "I've got some important info to tell the both of you." She stood back and stared at me. "I swanny. Are you sure you're not due till December?"

Molly interrupted, "She's carrying your grandbaby. You must be so excited, Grace."

I sat speechless.

"Of course." She snatched a scone off the tray, reached into my kitchen cabinet, and pulled out a dessert plate. "Did you make coffee, Molly?"

I couldn't hold back. "Grace, what did you want to tell us that's so important?" I crossed my arms in front of me and tapped my foot.

"Well, Rae, your hormones must be on overdrive. I'll forgive you for being so snippy." She sauntered to the coffee pot and poured herself a cup. "Mick Treavor's grandmother passed away and he and Lauren are flying to Wyoming. The Historical Society is in urgent mode. Plan 7-C is under way."

"What's 7-C?" I took a bite of egg.

"Rae, I gave you the handbook when you got back from your honeymoon. Guess you haven't had time to peruse the pages since you're so busy." She sipped her coffee and nibbled a scone.

Molly interjected. "Oh fiddlesticks, Grace. We already knew about Mick's grandma. Please tell Rae and me what 7-C is?"

My mom-in-law pulled a pamphlet out of her navy-blue bag. "There ya go." She pointed to 7-C. "1. Supply transportation to funeral locale. 2. Reserve hotel, if needed. 3. Order flowers or donate to charity of family's choice. 4. Care for extraneous needs. 5. Be available 24/7. The Historical Society is ready and waiting. We must help Lauren and Mick."

I sauntered to the fridge, snatched a plastic cup from the cupboard, then poured myself a glass of milk. "Grace, I've spoken to Lauren, and they have most of 7-C taken care of. I'll be glad to make sure all is well."

"It's in your hands. Please let me know what you find out." She swallowed the last of her coffee. "Ladies, that's not the only reason I came by. The Historical Society mailbox has received complaints about all the noise and machinery behind the Bed and Breakfast. I won't tell you who is complaining because you know her. Even though she doesn't live in Hope, she drives here for sweets from Bitty's Buns.

I tried to guess, but she kept chattering.

"I won't say another word except her last name starts with C, and her daughter's first name starts with M. I'll mention it at our next meeting." She finished her scone, "Better go y'all. Duty calls." She moseyed into the mud room, pulled her rain cap onto her frizzy do, and then the back door slapped shut behind her.

I was so glad I'd stuffed a piece of scone in my mouth. Otherwise, I'd have said something to my children's grandma that wasn't worth repeating.

The back door flew open, again, and Grace stood at the entryway to the kitchen. Hands on hips. "I forgot to mention we're inviting Lauren to join the Historical Society."

With that, she was out the door, down the steps, and gone. *Hallelujah!*

Molly and I stood mesmerized.

* * *

Joe came home for lunch. "Rae, is this the family lasagna recipe? Remember how I tricked you when we were dating?" He shoveled a mouthful of the Italian delight into his mouth.

"How could I forget." I rolled my eyes. "Recipe on the box. Family recipe, not!" I took a bite of crunchy salad greens. "How's your day been going?"

"It was great until my mom dropped by my office." He took a swig of sweet tea.

I put my fork down, "Why? Did it have anything to do with Mick's grandma and heavy equipment noise?"

"How'd you know?"

Poor fella never should have asked. "She came here today and told Molly and me about Mick's grandma passing. She said the Historical Society is going into 7-C mode."

"What's that?"

"Oh, husband of mine. You don't know? Haven't you read the Historical Society pamphlet explaining everything we ladies are to do in urgent situations?" I rolled my eyes.

He shoveled a fork full of meaty, cheesy pasta into his mouth, then washed it down with a swig of sweet tea. "I'm lost here. What are you talking about, Beautiful?"

"There's a list of great ideas to help in emergency situations. I suppose I should cut your mom some slack because she's trying to help Mick and Lauren. Grace also told us there are complaints about the loud machinery on our land. She hinted at who's writing the notes." I ate a mouthful of lasagna.

"Who needs phones when you've got my mom?" He laughed then wiped some rogue sauce off his chin. "Honey, I stopped by Tweeters Realty and spoke with Mick and Lauren. I told them I'll check periodically on the house they're having built. They thanked us for watching Heidi because she's their main concern." He took his last bite. "The noisy machinery complaint is crazy. Let's nip it in the bud." He paused and looked at my bare feet. "How about a field trip?" Crooked grin. "Might want to put on your boots."

"Boots?"

"Let's see how everything's going at the construction site. Are ya game?"

Shoes changed to boots, dogs let outside, Joe and I headed hand in hand to our land.

He will wipe every tear from their eyes. There will be no more death or mourning or crying or pain... Revelation 21:4

Chapter 3

We had purchased the land behind the Inn when Uncle Quinn's financial contribution made it possible, and we immediately became co-owners.

Fortunately for us, the team who'd renovated the Inn at Hope agreed to take on our new endeavor. Dr. Duntworth, the contractor, and Abel Dells, the architect, called Joe when they heard about our enterprise and said they had students who needed extra credit to graduate. Most work would be done pro-bono."

* * *

Heavy equipment engines roared, and hard-hat areas dotted the acreage.

Dr. Duntworth stood with one hand on a backhoe and the other hand signaled personnel. His hard hat teetered precariously on his noggin. He motioned for Joe and me to back up. "Good to see y'all but you need hard hats. Let's move over there." He gestured his chin toward a clearing.

Joe flicked a glob of red dirt off his pant leg. "How's it going, Dr. D? Need anything?"

"Bad weather slowed us down some." He grabbed a rag from his overall pocket and wiped his forehead. "Joe, your mom came by today and nearly fell into that mud over there." He pointed at a mountain of red dirt. "She told me folks are complaining about the noisy machinery."

Joe shook his head. "I heard. How can I help?"

"I'll take care of it. I called my wife and asked her to invite the Chandlers and your folks for dinner tonight. I know Mrs. Chandler is the complainer." He blew his nose on the rag and patted his ample stomach. "My wife's a great cook." He guffawed. "Food and fellowship mean no more complaints." He rolled up his sleeves. "Gotta get to work." He turned and ambled toward the heavy equipment. Enough said.

* * *

Joe changed from boots to shoes and headed back to the university. I slid into flip flops and strolled down Beaufort Street. Geranium, alyssum, and vinca filled pots lined the steps to Molly's Restaurant. I opened the door and noticed Joe's sister, Emily, in a favorite booth and moseyed in her direction. "Hey, Em. Mind if I join you?"

"Rae, of course you can join me." She smoothed her blonde hair into a ponytail. "I've ordered peach cobbler with two scoops of ice cream."

"I'm ordering that, too. I'm craving sweets."

"Blakey and I haven't found out the gender of the baby. I'm so antsy I just can't stand it, but we agreed to wait till birth. You know the nursery is pink, pink, and more-pink." She fiddled with her fork as furrows appeared between her brows.

"Are you okay?"

"I'm not. My feet are swollen and I'm not sleeping well. Plus, Roxie pup has allergies and keeps us awake at night and Blake keeps saying we might as well get used to no sleep because when the baby comes, we won't get any." She finally took a deep breath after the lengthy run-on sentence. "Plus, my hair is driving me crazy."

I stifled a laugh. "The good thing is, you and I will have babies only a month apart and we'll both be sleep deprived at the same time."

Molly approached our booth. "Good to see you ladies. Emily, I'll get your cobbler in a sec, sweet girl." She turned to me. "What would you like, my other expecting friend? Cobbler?"

"That sounds perfect. A la mode, of course, please."

"You two gals are spectacular. I love your frilly top, Emily; and Rae, your polka dots look adorable. Cherish this pregnancy time. Seems like yesterday I was expecting my girls." She snatched a napkin from her pocket, dabbed her eyes, and took our order to the counter.

Her hubby, Henry, waved to us as he scooped our desserts into bowls. He shuffled around the counter and set the deliciousness in front of us.

Emily and I spoke in unison, "Thank you, Henry."

He gave a thumbs up then wiped off a nearby booth.

I scooped a spoonful of cobbler and ice cream into my mouth and savored it for a few seconds. "Emily Wayne, I'm glad you're my sis-in-love."

"Aren't we just the most blessed gals in South Carolina?" She didn't wait for my response. "On second thought, Lauren must be included in the blessed gals club, too." She sniggled. "Did Mom tell you she wants Lauren to join the Hysterical Society? Since Lauren isn't pregnant, Mom will probably want her to head up the Fall Festival."

"She mentioned inviting Lauren." I closed my eyes and bit into the ooey gooey cobbler and ice cream. "Isn't it a little soon to get ready for the festival? It's only June now."

"Not really. Time flies and vendors need to be contacted." She devoured a spoonful of cobbler. "I need to talk with Lauren when she returns from her trip. She must learn to tell my mom no, otherwise, society stuff will dominate her calendar." She wiped a glob of peaches off her tiny baby bump. "Did you hear some folks are complaining about the noise from the heavy equipment? That's just ridiculous."

"It's all under control." I didn't dare share the dinner invite Dr. D divulged and darted to another topic, "Are you going to watch the Rodriguez kiddos after the baby comes?"

"I'll give it a try. Shelly told me not to stress. We'll make plans one day at a time. Since her parents live down in the valley, they can pick up the slack or watch the children full-time." She shoved a rogue hair in the ponytail. "That's it! I'm getting my hair cut."

Molly approached. "Need anything else, you two? Or is it you three, four, five, or more?"

Emily's eyes squinted. "Well, I swanny, Miss Molly, my baby bump only has room for one." She glanced at me, almost made a remark, and squelched it.

"Okay, my baby bump is larger. No need to bite your tongue, Emily." I rolled my eyes and patted her hand. "The more the merrier."

The bell above the restaurant jingled and in darted Grace. She spotted us, so our conversation never went any further. I could tell by Emily's goggle-eyed expression she wanted to ask about my comment. I bit my tongue, pursed my lips, and didn't make a peep. Until my mom-in-law scooted on the bench next to Emily.

I shoved my bowl away. "Hi, Grace." Cheshire cat grin.

Emily's mom fiddled with her hoop earrings. "So glad I caught you two. I know it's last minute, but Grady's home from his deployment and I've spoken to his wife, Izzy, and mom-in-law, Sea. We're planning a home-coming dinner to celebrate tomorrow. Plus, Uncle Quinn and Sendy arrive tomorrow afternoon from Texas. We're having barbeque for dinner. Y'all are invited. The Society ladies are bringing slaw, potato salad, and macaroni salad. Bring one of those. Preferably macaroni because that seems to be what the kids like."

Emily dabbed her mouth with a napkin. "Kids? Is this for all the neighbors or just our family?"

"Emily Byer Wayne, you know when we have a barbeque everyone's invited. I've already contacted folks to bring things. That's something you'll be doing when you start full time in the Society. It's a badge of honor to hold the coordinator position. I've already picked a job for Lauren."

I didn't mutter a word. Emily did.

"Mother, I'll do what I can, but you know this sweet baby gets my undivided attention." She rubbed her tummy. "By the way, what job have you chosen for Rae?"

I glared at my sister-in-law.

Molly meandered to our booth before Grace answered. "Here's your pecan pie, Grace. Hope you enjoy it."

Grace grinned, "I'm taking it to the Duntworth's tonight. Chandlers are going there for dinner, too. Should be interesting." She patted Emily's tummy and gave her a peck on the cheek. "Y'all take care." She strutted to the counter, paid Henry, and left with the pie in hand.

Emily and I said our goodbyes. She needed to go to the Rodriguez's before their children got home from day camp, and I wanted to stop at Sweetness and Sweaters to see Lauren's mom, Betty. I needed a mom hug.

* * *

The short jaunt to Sweetness and Sweaters filled my sense of sight with delight. Geraniums, petunias, alyssum, and ivy spilled over the sides of the window boxes on the historical shops and restaurants.

I pressed the door open to the adorable boutique and Betty greeted me with her usual, "Hey, sweet girl. It's so good to see you." She stepped from behind the counter and hugged my waist. "I've missed you, dear."

That's the hug I craved. Lauren's mother had told me I could call her mom, instead of Mom Wyatt. It tickled my heart pink to be cradled in her embrace. "I've missed you, too."

"Rae, how've you been feeling? You look fabulous!"

"I'm so big, though."

"You're carrying more than one, aren't you?" She winked.

"The first ultrasound showed one." I patted my tummy. "The one I just had showed two." Tears formed in my eyes. "I'm scared."

Betty wrapped her plump arms around my twin-sized waist. "Rae, God's got it. That's exciting news. Have you told Lauren?"

"Yes." I chortled. "I actually sat on her suitcase so she could close it this morning. I told her the babies were helping."

"You and my Lauren have such a bond. I'm so glad you saw her today. I'm saddened about Mick's grandma passing, but we know she's in heaven." Betty took my hand and guided me toward a clothing rack near the two dressing rooms. "Dear, come see what just arrived. Sendy ordered them before she left for Texas. She figured with all the marriages happening, babies might follow. By the way, did you hear that Fran's expecting. She thought Olivia was her caboose. But surprise! She's due in February."

"I hadn't heard. I'm thrilled for Fran and George!"

I sorted through the clothing and tried on a topaz-colored tea-length dress. The stretchy fabric allowed for expansion. "I love this." Twirl. "I just might need some new shoes."

"You are beautiful, Rae. We have just the pair for you." She held up a low-heeled wedge shoe. "This color is perfect."

Comfort. "These are fabulous."

I gazed at a few more items before paying. Betty placed my new shoes in the bottom of the bag, wrapped my dress in paisley tissue paper, then added it on top of the shoe box.

"Enjoy your goodies, Rae."

"How much do I owe you?"

"Not a thing, dear. It's a gift from me to you and the babies." She hugged my neck and shooed me out the door. "Rest well tonight."

A person finds joy in giving an apt reply—and
how good is a timely word! Proverbs 15:23

Chapter 4

I practically skipped home with the colorful bag swinging with every step. I pushed open the back gate and opened the screen door. Buddy and the two puppies flapped their ears in tandem as Puffs saddled to my side. "Come here you doggone, dogs." I ruffled their ears until my phone buzzed.

Uncle Quinn. "Hey, niece, last-minute request. Sendy and I need a cottage if you have one. We'll be there tomorrow."

"We have several. It'll be good to see you newlyweds."

Uncle Q whispered, "Can you do me a favor?" He didn't wait for my answer. "If you have more cottages, I need them."

"You sound very mysterious. Everything okay?"

He cleared his throat. Loudly. "Yep. Sendy's kids and mine are going to Hope. They've never met."

"Your kids?" *I didn't know you had any. Joe's never mentioned them.*

He belted out a cough. "Long story. No problem. They can stay in Greenville."

"Uncle Q, all the bungalows are available. Our last guests checked out after Lauren's wedding. How many do you need?"

"All of 'em." He grumbled something indecipherable. "Thanks." Call ended.

I grabbed an apple off the kitchen counter and crunched and munched it to the core. While sitting at the historical desk and adding Uncle Q and Sendy's families to the reservation list, I glanced at a picture on the wall. I loved the photo of my grandparents and Joe's grandparents at the bed and breakfast many years ago. *Grandma and Grandpa, I'm so thankful you gave me an inheritance so I could buy this bed and breakfast.* My thoughts were short-lived when the front doors to the Inn opened.

Collette Timble peeked around the open door. "Anybody home?"

Her sing-song voice made me giggle and answer in kind. "Come on in, Collette and baby Daisy. Rae is here being a little lazy."

She stepped through the foyer and into the check-in area. "You silly girl." Collette attempted to lean over the antique desk to give me a hug then began to teeter forward with baby Daisy on her hip.

"Just a sec, I'm coming around the desk to hug y'all. It's so good to see you two."

"Rae, you look fabulous! I can't wait to hear about the pregnancy. How are you doing?"

"I'm doing---."

The screen door burst open and Collette's husband, Earnest, stumbled into the foyer. "Sorry for the grand entrance, ladies, but I've got my hands full." He shoved a suitcase inside with one foot, held a baby carrier in one arm, and another suitcase in the other. A diaper bag slung across his back.

Collette handed me Daisy and darted to help Earnest. "Honey, we don't even know if Rae has a cottage. You should've left everything in the car."

My mind reeled. *I hate to tell them all the cottages are reserved.* "How many nights do y'all need?" I snuggled Daisy.

Collette's brow furrowed. "Rae, this is so last minute. Dr. D and Mr. Dells said everything is a go for the splash pad and, as you know, Earnie's team oversees that. I decided to tag along. We'll be here at least a month."

Earnest set the baby carrier and suitcase down while Collette rescued the diaper bag before it fell on the floor.

I pointed to a couple of chairs. "Just scoot everything over there. Y'all can stay in the family cottage this evening." I handed Daisy to Collette "Uncle Quinn reserved all the bungalows starting tomorrow evening. Not sure how long he'll need them." I closed the laptop. "Everything will work out, though. I'm so glad you're here."

Earnest hadn't heard a word I'd said because his phone was practically attached to his ear. He muted it then kissed Collette's cheek. "I'm going to the land to do a walk through."

Daisy started crying and rubbing her eyes with her pudgy fist. Collette plopped into a nearby chair. "She needs to eat. Mind if I nurse her?"

"Please make yourself at home. Of course, I don't mind. Poor thing is starving." I shuffled to the kitchen. "Collette, I don't want the dogs to be a nuisance, so I'll take them outside." *I really want time to call Joe in private.*

"Please don't. We want a dog and Daisy needs to get used to the extra noise and attention."

"Okay, then. While you're caring for Daisy, I'll unlock the family cottage for y'all."

She gave a thumbs up and cradled Daisy.

* * *

I texted Joe.

Me: Earnest and family are here and want a cottage for a month.

I waited a minute or two for his response.

Joe: Knew Earnest was coming. Why concern? Cottages are open.

Me: Uncle Q reserved all cottages starting tomorrow.

Joe: Why? How long?

Me: Sendy's home's being renovated. Her kids and Uncle Q's are coming. Don't know how long.

Joe: Haven't seen Q's kids since I was small.

Me: Why not?

Joe: I'll explain later.

Me: Timble's staying in fam cottage tonight. No room rest of month. Let's invite them to dinner at Molly's.

Joe: Great idea. Be home soon.

I pushed open the bungalow door and did a quick inspection. Everything looked pristine and ready for tonight's guests.

* * *

Baby Daisy slept soundly in her carrier while Collette and I sipped glasses of icy lemonade in the comfy office chairs. My three hounds and Lauren's nestled nearby in the foyer.

"Collette, I'm so glad you and the baby came with Earnest. You can give me some pointers on motherhood."

"Well, obviously I'm not the one to give advice. I insisted Earnest bring us without thinking it through and now my daughter won't be in her familiar crib or anything." She sniffled.

I almost used the word "hormones" like Joe's mom did to me earlier, but I caught myself before the words even touched my lips.

"You know what it teaches me?"

She shook her head. "What?"

"If there's a time Joe takes a trip for work and I have the option of going, I am. That's something you taught me without even knowing it. Family time is important."

"Guess I didn't think of it like that."

"Would y'all like to have dinner with Joe and me at Molly's tonight?"

"I'll answer for Ernie and me. We'd love to."

...Rather, in humility value others above
yourselves, not looking to your own interests
but each of you to the interests of the others.
Philippians 2:3-4

Chapter 5

The restaurant bustled. Molly's specials always brought a crowd and tonight was no exception. Joe and Earnest pushed tables together when Emily and Blake joined us.

Joe drew my chair closer to his then sat next to me and whispered, "You look ravishing, lovely wife." He leaned in and smooched my cheek. Then he joined Blake and Earnest in a conversation about the splash pad.

Emily cooed at baby Daisy while she and Collette were deep in conversation. I missed Lauren already. She and I would have chitter-chattered while our fellas talked. *Joe's mom might be right. Hormones?*

My dad-in-love, Lance Byer, pushed through the front door to Molly's Restaurant and scuttled in our direction. "Hey girls." He beamed at the sight of Emily and me. "You two mommas taking care of yourselves? Hmmm, maybe I should ask Joe and Blake if they're taking care of you." He jokingly punched Joe's shoulder and pointed to Blake. "I'm keeping an eye on you fellas. Remember, those are my grandbabies, so you'd better pamper your wives."

Grace side-stepped him. "I swanny, Lance. Tilly and Gentry are already here, and Emily and Blake's baby is their grandchild, too. Quit being stingy." She wove between a couple chairs then stopped when she heard Lance's words.

"Wait a minute, Granny Grace."

She made an about-face, glowered at her husband, then turned and darted around tables toward the back of the dining area. He jokingly tiptoed behind her. *My dad would have liked my dad-in-love.*

Only one entrée was served this evening with all the fixins'. Mouth-watering fried chicken, mashed potatoes, fried okra, green beans, cream corn, and cornbread filled each person's plate.

Joe licked his fingers after delving into a chicken leg and stuffing a gravy-laden mashed potato bite into his mouth. He broke off a piece of cornbread and slathered it with creamy butter.

I stifled a giggle. "Here, Hunk." I handed him a napkin. "Looks like you're enjoying your meal." Wink. I love that man!

* * *

Collette, Daisy, and Earnest moseyed back to their cottage as Joe and I strolled hand in hand across the brick street toward the lake. Our favorite bench sat waiting for our arrival. Joe proposed to me on that bench, and months after our wedding I told him I was pregnant on the exact spot.

"Beautiful, where are the Timbles staying after tonight?"

"Do you have any suggestions? Collette feels so bad because she insisted on coming, and now they don't have a place to stay. If we can come up with an idea, that might ease her mind. Poor thing is taking care of Dixie and Earnest. She seems stressed." I nuzzled into the crook of Joe's arm. "What if I'm the same way when our babies arrive?"

Joe squeezed my hand. "We'll work it out together. No worries."

"Thanks, Joseph."

Joe sat straight as an arrow. "I have an idea, but it'll involve Mick and Lauren."

"Mick and Lauren?"

"Mick told me Lauren's house is up for rent. He asked if I'd let him know if anyone might be interested while they're away."

He drummed his chin with his fingers. "Timbles need a house for a month. Maybe they'll lease it to them."

"That's a brilliant idea! I wish I'd thought of it!"

"I'll text Mick."

"If they say yes, we'll let the Timbles know. At least they'll have an option regardless of their decision."

Joe sent a text. No response.

* * *

We traipsed home, changed into our boots, got the four dogs, and walked to the land behind the Inn.

"Joe, why haven't you seen Uncle Q's kids since you were small? I always dreamed of having cousins. I can't imagine not seeing them."

He squeezed my hand. "It wasn't intentional. Uncle Quinn made some bad choices earlier in his life, Aunt Rosie divorced him, remarried, and moved to Europe with my cousins. That's all I know." He shrugged. "Mom knows the details."

I stopped, shielded my eyes from the sun with my free hand, and looked up at my hubby. "It's good you'll see them again and I'll get to meet them."

Buddy pulled at his leash and led the pack with his gargantuan nose sniffing every squirrel filled tree. We peeked inside the windows of a couple buildings under renovation and surveyed the rest of the area. When we rounded the dilapidated large building, Puffs' guttural sound startled me. Buddy growled, and the puppies joined in the ruckus. I zoomed behind Joe, and he laughed uncontrollably.

"Rae, look why the hounds are going crazy. You're not going to believe it." He gently pulled me from my hiding place behind him.

The culprit. Heavy equipment with Midnight, my neighbor's cat, teetering on the tip-top of the machinery.

"Should we call Miss Doris? Poor Midnight will never get down."

"She doesn't have a phone. I'll go ahead and call the fire station. Maybe they'll tell us how to lure her cat." Joe patted the dogs' heads and shushed them. He made the call.

* * *

The truck arrived with sirens blaring. Joe pointed to the top of the crane. Val's nephew, who was a vet student and volunteer fireman, climbed the ladder. Kramer jumped off the last ladder rung with Midnight holding onto him for dear life. Neither Joe nor I noticed the crowd behind us until we heard enthusiastic cheering.

Joe turned and waved to the Hope-ites. "What are y'all doing here?" He laughed. "Dumb question—."

Emily tapped her foot on the red clay. "Big brother, you know anytime we hear a siren we're on the scene."

Kramer put Midnight in a carrier then Joe shook his hand. "Nice going, Kram. I don't mind taking Midnight to Doris."

"She's been taken to the hospital in Greenville."

Grace pressed forward with Historical Society members at her heals. "Ladies, Plan 4-B is in effect."

Emily and I were newbies to the society and had no idea what Plan 4-B meant.

Before anyone said another word, Kramer removed his coat. He held his phone. "Excuse me, I have to make a call."

Opal, the historian, got out her phone. "I'll call Val."

Kramer pointed to his phone. "I'm talking to her. I'll deliver Midnight to my aunt."

Opal gave a thumbs up. "I'll call Anne and Lottie to let them know we're all on alert."

Anne tapped her shoulder and Lottie spoke loudly. "No need. We're all here. We heard the siren and had to see what was happening. We are informed ladies."

Victoria, the parliamentarian and mayor's wife, waved her phone in the air. "Hey, y'all. Doris is on the phone. Quiet down, please." She listened intently. The double vertical lines on her forehead told us this was serious. She raised her hand in the air. "Quiet, everybody. She's broken her hip and will have surgery."

Grace leaned closer to Victoria to hear the conversation. Then the other ladies did the same. When the call ended, we all knew Doris needed more than Plan 4-B. Whatever that was. She needed all the help we could muster.

Plans fail for lack of counsel, but with many advisers they succeed. Proverbs 15:22

Chapter 6

Nightmares flooded my mind throughout the night. I awoke twisted between the sheets with my tangled hair strewn across the pillow. I patted the pillow next to mine, opened my eyes, and saw that Joe wasn't there. Four whining dogs pressed open the bedroom door and almost lured me out of bed. Until I heard a groan outside the bedroom from Joe. I shamefully closed my eyes and pretended to be asleep.

Joe followed close behind the dogs. "Shush." He whispered. "Y'all get downstairs."

I couldn't squelch a giggle and opened my eyes. "Joseph William Byer, what are you doing? Aren't you late for work?" I unwrapped myself from the covers, stepped out of bed, and sauntered in his direction. The four dogs prevented me from getting close to my hubby. So, I blew him a kiss.

"That's not going to do the trick, Mrs. Byer." He pointed toward the dogs. "Downstairs, you mongrels." My swashbuckling husband swung his arms in jest. But it worked. Puffs and Buddy started to lead their pups into the living room and Joe side stepped, wrapped me in his arms, and planted a smooch on my lips. "No, Mrs. Rae, I'm not late for work. I took the day off."

"What? I can't believe it." I spun into his arms. "What about the Timbles? They need breakfast. Plus, they have to check out today."

"As usual, Chef Molly has everything under control. They're eating breakfast downstairs right now. I just spoke with them."

"Joe, I had nightmares all night about Collette, Earnest, and Daisy wandering the streets and looking for a place to stay."

"Well, wife of mine, they do have a place to stay." He raked his fingers through his hair. "Mick called and said he and Lauren are staying in his house when they get back from Wyoming while they wait for their home to be built. Timbles can rent Lauren's house.

"That's fabulous! I'll rest much better tonight. No nightmares." I stretched my arms above my head. "How did Mick sound?"

"Tired. It's good he has Lauren to lean on." He tapped my head with his finger. "I know how important you are to me. It's good he has a spouse."

"You sweet man. I'm glad you feel that way. So do I."

"You need to get dressed, Beautiful. I'm taking you out for brunch."

"Yes, Sir!" Awkward salute. "Wait a minute, we can't go anywhere. Uncle Quinn, Sendy, and their brood will be here this afternoon."

Joe opened the doors to our domain and the dogs charged ahead. He blurted over his shoulder, "I've already done a walk-through and all the cottages are ready. No worries. By the way, Kramer's coming to the Inn to study the dogs for one of his veterinary courses plus..." He caught himself mid-sentence. "Kelly is coming to the Inn for the day because she wants to use the kitchen to make something for the barbeque tonight."

"Who's going to check everybody in when they get here?"

"Kelly. No worries."

"I'm glad they're dating. Maybe when they graduate and have good jobs they'll marry." I traipsed into the bathroom and called over my shoulder. "I'm glad you proposed to me, Hubby."

"Me, too."

* * *

The VW Bug cruised toward Greenville. "Joseph, you're being quite mysterious. I hope what I'm wearing is appropriate."

"You know my favorite color is orange. You look stunning."

* * *

We dined in an enclosed porch at a tiny bistro overlooking the Reedy River. Quaint. Each table cozied near the windows for a gorgeous view of the flowing water.

"Thank you, Joe. I didn't even know this little gem existed."

"Think about it. You've been running the bed and breakfast since you got to South Carolina and haven't had time to go to Greenville much."

"Well, I'll have you know, I do know where Burger King is." I sniggled and eased into my chair. "By the way, I made macaroni salad for the barbeque tonight. Let's make sure we're home in plenty of time for me to change before the meal." I sipped my herbal tea.

"No need. Molly's taking it for us."

I peered over the rim of my cup, "Why?"

"We're not going."

"What?"

"We're staying in Greenville tonight. We need time as a couple before the babies come and this seemed like the only time we'll have. Since I take over dad's position at the university next week, we'll be swamped. Kramer's staying overnight at the Inn and watching the hound dogs." He put his fork down. "Maybe I should've asked you first?"

"Nope, I love this surprise! Is your mom okay with it? You know how she wants everyone at the barbeque." I squirmed.

"It's all good."

I hope so.

* * *

The bell hop transported our items to a suite on the top floor of a fancy schmancy hotel. Roses, in the shape of a heart sat between the pillows on the luxurious king-sized bed. Breathtaking.

"Joseph, this is gorgeous." I sighed. "It's too much."

He put his finger to his lips. "It's never too much when it comes to you."

Room service. Dinner by candlelight. Old movie playing. Chocolate eclairs for dessert.

It seemed a little weird that our fur babies weren't snuggled with us. But I must admit, this moment nestled in Joe's embrace--heavenly.

Dear children, let us not love with words or
speech but with actions and truth. 1 John 3:18

Chapter 7

After traveling the winding road from Greenville to Hope, we parked at the Inn, and went inside. I moseyed upstairs.

Joe walked straight through the foyer and opened the back door. He laughed as he watched Kramer and the dogs darting back and forth in the yard. "Hey, Kramer, I see they have you under control. Thanks for helping Rae and me."

Kramer wiped his hands on his shirt. "I had a great time. Whenever y'all need me to watch them, I'll do it."

"Follow me." Joe motioned.

Kramer stepped inside as the canines inched close behind. He stood in the mud room.

"Come into the kitchen."

"No, sir. My boots are muddy. I'm good."

Joe pulled cash from his pocket and handed it to him. "You'll be a terrific Vet. Thanks, Kram."

"Thank you, Professor Byer." He patted the heads of P, B, T, and H and exited the back door.

* * *

Joe dashed upstairs to help unpack our bags. "Kramer did a great job, Honey. He'll be available whenever we need him."

"I'm glad cuz we might need a few more getaway times before the babies come." I stood on tiptoe and kissed his chin.

"Definitely." He leaned down for a smooch then paused mid-kiss at the sound of cheering outside our open upstairs window. "What in the world?"

We leaned on the sill and noticed Uncle Quinn wearing his black Stetson and sitting atop a Morgan horse.

An audience of cottage dwellers gawked at the real Texas cowboy as he shouted in our direction. "Joe and Rae, this is one of the horses that'll be stabled for the kids to ride. She's a beaut. Come on down here. Y'all have had enough alone time."

Joe and I tromped downstairs and out the front doors to where cowboy Quinn sat proudly upon his steed. I noticed Sendy exiting their cottage. She sashayed to Uncle Q, held onto his hand, and he pulled her onto the back of the horse.

Quinn guided the animal in front of all the cottages then led him back to where Joe and I stood. "What do ya think?"

Joe and I gave a thumbs up.

Sendy slid off the massive animal. "Rae, I love the idea of living part-time here and in Texas." She pointed to Uncle Quinn. "That man would live in a stable if I agreed to it." She winked. "That's never happening!" She took my hand and whispered. "By the way, Molly and I chatted about you today." She patted my tummy. "More than one baby?"

"Uh-huh."

"You'll be a great mom, dear. Now come see my family and meet Quinn's. They want to make the Inn at Hope a family tradition. We'd like to gather here once a year for a reunion. Do ya mind?"

"I love that idea!" I sauntered toward the farthest cottages with Sendy and noticed Joe engrossed in a conversation with Uncle Q.

* * *

Evening fast approached. Uncle Quinn and Sendy opted for a meal with Grace and Lance. They dined at Fenster Haus, a greenhouse transformed into a classy restaurant, located across from the lake.

Joe rounded up his cousins for supper, who were officially mine now, and they crowded into cars and paraded behind our Bug to Gill's. This eclectic burger haven was a favorite spot of ours.

The line of cousins and their children swirled in rope-like fashion from the parking lot to the front door of the restaurant. My Professor and I stood at the front of the line.

Lou pushed open the entry door to the eatery and shouted, "Tables available for Joe, Rae, and the twenty-four folks with them. Enter at your own risk. Walk, don't run!" He pretended to shield himself from the onslaught of customers as Joe and I motioned for all to follow.

We filled the entire back room. The overhead fans spun and almost nipped the tip of Cousin Melvin's cowboy hat. Joe scooted toward the end of the table nearest Quinn's off-spring so he could visit the cousins he hadn't seen in ages.

I squeezed between Sendy's daughter-in-law, Candy, and Lucia, Quinn's daughter. The loud chatter amongst the group made me pause. I'd never dreamed my family would ever be this big or this loud. I loved it.

The servers took our orders and delivered each meal with finesse. They never skipped a beat as they moved in time to a trendy song on the juke box and balanced each serving tray with ease.

Melvin clanked his glass with a spoon to get the families' attention, then nodded at Joe. "Mind if I return thanks, Cuz?"

Joe nodded. He took my hand in his, and we bowed as Melvin prayed and ended with a hearty "Amen" from all of us.

Emily scooched her chair closer to Lucia and me. "I heard y'all might have a reunion here every year. I sure hope it's true." She jammed a chili-coated fry into her mouth and wiped a rogue glob from her chin.

Lucia pushed a strand of chocolate brown hair behind her ear. "Sendy and Dad are planning this reunion thing. I'm not sure I'll be able to come each year, but I'm glad I got to this time." She pointed at four teenage girls sitting with three younger boys at a picnic table outside on the deck. "Those four gals and three fellas are Melvin's and mine."

Emily glared. "You have seven children?"

"We do." Lucia whispered. "As a matter of fact, number eight will be arriving in a week. We've adopted a four-year-old boy."

Emily gawked. "Eight children? You deserve a badge of courage." She patted her baby bump. "I'm having my first near Thanksgiving. I might call you for baby advice if you don't mind."

Lucia grinned from ear to ear. "Maybe we can help each other out."

Emily squirmed. "What do you mean? I'll be a new mom and haven't a clue what I'm doing." Her fingers nervously drummed the edge of the table.

"Emily, I don't need help with children." She patted Em's hand. "Did you think I was going to ask you to babysit my kiddos or something?" Lucia said in jest, then crunched a bite of dill pickle.

Emily, gulped. "Then what do you want me to do?"

"Talk to your mom." She pushed her empty plate to the side.

"Why?" Emily scooted closer to her cousin.

"Aunt Grace is trying to convince my dad to live in Hope permanently. I love her to bits, but she doesn't realize how much we cherish Dad living in Texas. Mel and I live in Fredericksburg which is about 50 miles from him, and our kids absolutely adore their Papa Quirky."

Emily bit her lip. "Lucia, it's so important for you to see your daddy. I can't imagine mine living far away."

"The last time I lived close to my dad was when I was little. I know Sendy and Dad made a compromise of half a year in S.C. and the other half in Texas. I can't stand the thought of him being so far all year long." She gulped her water. "Now that he's co-owner of the land near the Inn, Aunt Grace thinks he should manage it. That's probably what they're discussing at the restaurant." She looked at me. "No offense, Rae, my aunt thinks you and Joe will be swamped with the baby coming and running the Inn at Hope."

I didn't say a word because Emily did. "Lucia, I'm so glad you let me know. I'll help." She looked at me. "No worries, Sis."

"I'm not worried, Em." Then I turned to Lucia. "What you said makes a lot of sense--."

Emily popped from her seat. "Excuse me girls. I'm going out to the deck to talk to your kids, Lucia. After all, we are family." She zigzagged between the tables, saw her hubby Blake along the way, planted a kiss on his cheek, and headed outside.

Lucia relaxed in her chair. "I know Emily and I are related, but I don't have nearly as much energy as that girl. Guess I didn't inherit the Energizer gene."

"No one has as much energy as Em." I laughed.

* * *

Joe and I went home, snuggled on the living room sectional, and shared a bowl of ice cream. "Joseph. I'm thrilled we got to spend time with all your family. It'll be fun if they come every year for a reunion."

"They're your family, too."

"I'm so glad."

"Me, too."

Carry each other's burdens, and in this way you will fulfill the law of Christ. Galatians 6:2

Chapter 8

Morning arrived in all its sunshiny glory. A glass of cold milk and a bagel schmeared with strawberry cream cheese sat on the nightstand by my side of the bed. *Joseph, you spoil me.* My phone buzzed, I snatched it off the side table, flipped my feet out of bed and onto the wooden floor. "Joe, is everything okay?"

"It is. Have lunch with me today?"

I rubbed my eyes and yawned. "What time?"

"I'll pick you up at noon. Love you."

"Love you, Hunk. Bye."

My phone buzzed again. "Emily, how are you doing?"

"I'm fine. Mom's in Greenville for the day. She's doing some retail therapy because she's scared about dad's retirement. She's afraid their lives will get boring." She paused. "Well, let me get to the point. Since Mom's out of town, we're calling an urgent meeting of the Historical Society ladies without telling her."

"What's up?"

"Victoria, Lottie, Anne, and Opal are planning a surprise luncheon for Mom this week since she's been Daddy's right-hand lady all these years at the university and since he's retiring." She sniggled. "Of course, you know Daddy's retiring since Joe is taking his job." Chuckle. "What do ya think?"

"Great idea. When's the meeting?"

"Twelve today at Bitty's Buns. Everyone's supposed to walk to the bakery. We'll be as discreet as possible because you know

this small town. Word spreads like muscadine jam on bread."
Call ended.

I sent Joe a text:

Me: Historical ladies mtng. Can't do lunch

Joe: Rain check?

Me: Yes. Heart emoji

Joe: Love you

Me: PS: planning surprise for your mom. Will fill you in later

* * *

I showered, wound my hair into one thick braid, and put on a butter yellow summer dress. My sand-colored flip flops slipped on easily. I added a silver necklace with the baby shoe charm Joe had surprised me with when I told him I was pregnant. My insightful hubby already knew.

The canines sat side by side and watched me as I did a slow twirl in front of the bedroom mirror and put on tangerine lip gloss. Then they led the way downstairs. I paused in the foyer and giggled at the sight of my four-legged babies, then twirled again. "How do I look?" Buddy flopped his ears, Puffs did the best doggy smile I'd seen, and their two puppies yawned. "You sweet things, I'm hoping your responses mean okay."

The knock on the front doors put the dogs in a tizzy and startled me. My eyes bulged when I saw my mother-in-law standing on the porch. "Grace." My stunned expression halted her in her tracks. "Everything okay?"

She stepped inside and the screen door slapped shut behind her. "Rae, I swanny, that baby has to be farther along than the doctor said." She pulled a tissue from her white crop pant pocket and dotted the beads of perspiration on her brow. "Never mind that. Do you have any water? I'd prefer bottled."

No, Mrs. Grace Byer, we don't have water in our home. Maybe you should go down to the lake and draw a bucket for yourself. "Let me get you a glass. Please have a seat."

"No thanks. I don't have time. I'm going to Greenville to shop and thought Quinn and Sendy might want to go, but they're not at their cottage. I thought they'd be in here. I had something pressing to tell him."

I let the dogs outside, shuffled into the kitchen, then filled a goblet with ice and bottled water. "Here you go, Grace. I'm not sure where Uncle Quinn and Sendy are. We don't require guests to ask permission to leave." I nervously giggled. "You know I'm just kidding?"

"This isn't a time to joke. This is serious." She guzzled her drink, darted into the kitchen, snatched dish soap from under the sink, and proceeded to wash her goblet.

"Grace, I can do that."

She shook her head, pulled a cotton dishtowel from the drawer nearest the sink, and dried the crystal. "Spit spot perfect." After placing the goblet into the cabinet and wiping off the droplets of water around the sink, she trotted to the front door with hands in her pockets. "Guess I'll head to Greenville by myself. TaTa."

I stood at the front doors, watched the Historical Society President jump into her SUV and peel rubber down the driveway. *I have no clue what you were talking about, Madam President.*

...not giving up meeting together, as some are
in the habit of doing, but encouraging one
another... Hebrews 10:25

Chapter 9

The CLOSED sign dangled on the front door to Bitty's Buns. I stood outside the bakery and sent a text to Emily to find out if our meeting place had changed.

Me: Still mtng at Bitty's?

Emily: No answer

Instead, she opened the front door to the bakery, peered from left to right, then motioned me inside. "Rae, what took you so long? You're fifteen minutes late."

The hysterical ladies sat at the long table near the back. Victoria waved then pointed to an empty seat with my name plate on the table in front of it. "Sit here, dear. No need to explain your lateness."

I flopped onto the wooden chair. "Ladies, I have a good excuse."

Lottie folded her hands on the table. "What is it, Rae?"

"Grace came by the Inn looking for Uncle Quinn and Sendy. She had something important to tell them. Then she said she was going to Greenville by herself."

Anne snickered. "I wonder if she suspects something. We can't ever surprise Grace with anything--."

"Isn't that the truth?" Emily blurted. "Remember when Blake and I thought we'd surprise our moms about the pregnancy, and they knew already?"

Victoria cleared her throat. "We remember, but that's not our focus now. I need a volunteer to watch the front door."

Natalie raised her hand, "I'll do it since I'll be going back and forth anyway." She delivered egg salad and pimento cheese sandwiches on two hot pink platters. "You gals need sustenance for this endeavor. I'll get y'all pitchers of lemonade and sweet tea."

"Thanks, Natalie." We softly said in unison.

She scampered to the counter to get our drinks. Then halted in her tracks. "Shush." She crouched down and practically duck walked to where we all sat. "Grace's SUV just parked out front. If she sees the closed sign we're finished. She'll really be suspicious."

Emily pulled her phone from her purse and called Grace. "Mother, how's it going?" She placed a finger to her lips and glared at us. Then she put the phone on speaker.

We heard Grace's voice. "How's it going? What in the world is going on? I'm in front of Bitty's Buns, and there's a closed sign out front. Do you know what's happening? I know something's up."

Emily motioned for us to get under the table. We didn't. There was no way the older women in the group and my pregnant belly for two could crawl on all fours under the doggone thing.

My sister-in-love muted her phone. "Ladies, I don't know what to do. My mother is as stubborn as an ox."

Natalie tapped her shoulder. "I'm going out the back door and nonchalantly meet her out front. I'll blubber some excuse as to why the bakery is closed. Then I'll go with her to Greenville or wherever she wants to go. I could use a break anyway." Natalie whispered to Emily. "Just keep chatting with your mom otherwise she might pick the front door lock with a bobby pin or something to snoop inside for clues." She patted Em's arm, stealthily moved toward the counter at the front of the tiny bakery, grabbed her purse, giggled, then headed out the back door.

We all remained silent until a text from Natalie to Emily appeared.

Natalie: Going to Greenville (smiley face emoji)
Emily: Thumbs up emoji

* * *

All the ladies spoke over each other until Victoria tapped her water glass with a spoon. "Ladies. Quiet. Please." A few seconds of silence filled the room. "We're getting nowhere and we're on limited time. Any suggestions as to the date?" The room filled with chatter again. "One at a time, please." She bit into her pimento cheese sandwich.

Lottie raised her hand like a schoolgirl. "Teacher Victoria, I suggest we do this as soon as possible and tell her our society meeting is at Fenster Haus."

Anne interrupted. "She might be suspicious if we meet at Fenster Haus unless we do it on Sunday after church." She paused. "Come to think of it, that won't work. The retirement will have already occurred."

Opal raised both hands in jest. "We can still have the luncheon at Fenster Haus on a different day. But how can we get Grace there without her expecting anything?"

We muddled over a stealth plan for the surprise party for almost two hours, then realized we hadn't contacted Fenster Haus to find out if the restaurant was available.

Victoria called, "Shelly, the society ladies are putting together a surprise retirement party for Grace, and we'd like to invite all the ladies in town. Would y'all have anything available in two days? I know it's last minute." She cleared her throat. "Mind if I put you on speaker?"

"That's just fine." She laughed. "Hey, ladies! I don't even need to check the calendar. The only large group we have this week arrives from Walhalla in a few minutes. We'll discuss details later if you don't mind."

Victoria chortled. "Thank you so much, Shelly."

Opal popped out of her chair, "Ladies, I have an idea how we can get Grace to Fenster Haus...

"Ladies, quiet please." Emily's phone buzzed. "I just got a text from my mom."

Grace: Back from Greenville. Dropping Natalie off at the bakery in a few. Need you to notify the society ladies for an emergency meeting right now at Natalie's. Have new info about Miss Doris and her cat. Hurry! Time is of the essence.

Emily: Will send a text to all

My sister-in-love tossed her phone into her backpack. "Exit out the back everybody. Let's disperse in different directions. Then enter Bitty's Buns through the front door at different times like we're getting here for the first time."

Victoria grabbed her purse as Emily and I cleared the sandwich plates from the table and put them behind the counter. The other ladies wiped the community table and pushed chairs in place.

We scampered out the back door of the bakery, through the graveled road behind the shops, and dispersed.

A word was secretly brought to me, my ears
caught a whisper of it. Job 4:12

Chapter 10

Grace tapped her gavel and brought us all to order. She never suspected the Historical Society ladies had held a meeting prior to this one. "Doris isn't well. Her surgery is tomorrow morning, and her daughter arrives in Hope tonight. She's staying at a hotel near the hospital."

Natalie placed water glasses in front of us. "If you girls need anything, just let me know."

Grace proceeded. "I've already spoken to Val about Doris's cat. Midnight is healthy, just a little stressed." She sipped her water. "I also spoke to Doris's daughter, Hazel. After surgery and rehab, Doris will move to Kansas to live with her. Midnight can't make the trip because Hazel and her children are allergic to cats."

Anne interjected. "So, what's the plan?"

Grace raised her voice an octave or two. "Anyone want to have Midnight for their very own?"

Silence.

Grace folded her arms, "Come on ladies, someone needs to step up to the plate."

With that remark almost everyone spoke in unison. "How about you, Grace?" I didn't say a word.

Grace fumbled with her answer. "You know I'm allergic to felines. At least I think I am."

Before I could squelch myself, I blurted. "How about Izzy? Remember how her little ones hugged Midnight when they

46

stayed at one of the cottages. I can't remember which of her kiddos made the comment that they wanted a pet when their daddy got home. Well, Grady's home now and I don't think they've gotten a dog, cat, guinea pig, or anything for that matter."

Emily affirmed. "You're right, Sis. They'd be perfect."

Grace pulled her phone from her bag. "I'll call Izzy with the news."

Natalie clutched a pitcher of water in her hands as she scuttled closer to the table. "I know I'm not a member of the society, but I couldn't help but overhear y'all. Wouldn't it be better if you asked Doris or her daughter if it would be okay to contact Izzy?" She placed the water flask on the table.

My mother-in-law dropped her phone into her purse. "Guess you're right. I'll call Hazel since Doris doesn't have a phone."

We all nodded in agreement.

Grace contacted Hazel who sat in the hospital room with Doris. The message was relayed, and Hazel said to contact Izzy. We heard Doris in the background. "Please take care of my kitten. My heart aches that I won't be able to keep her."

My heart, and I believe everyone else's, broke into little pieces at the sound of Doris weeping. The call ended.

Grace called Izzy and put her phone on speaker mode. She and Grady agreed to take Midnight into their home. They promised to stop by the hospital soon and stand near the window outside Doris' room. They'd cradle Midnight and let Miss Doris see how much love they'd give her kitty.

Grace motioned for all of us to quit chattering. "Ladies, now that Midnight will be fine, who volunteers to set up a food calendar for Hazel?"

Victoria raised her hand, "Won't it be a little difficult to deliver meals to the hospital. I mean, I don't mind doing it, Grace, but I remember when Lance was there, it was easier for you to eat at the cafeteria." She hesitated. "I'll call Hazel and find out what works best for her. Do y'all agree?"

Grace gave a thumbs up then we all responded, "We agree."

*If either of them falls down, one can help the
other up... Ecclesiastes 4:10*

Chapter 11

I awoke early to the sound of heavy equipment engines. *I sure hope no one else complains about the noise.* After freshening up, I slipped into a kiwi hued linen sun dress and slip-on sandals. I twisted my hair into a Dutch braid then put on tiny teardrop shaped emerald earrings I'd inherited from my grandma.

I moseyed downstairs, only to be greeted by Puffs, Buddy, Trixie, and Heidi. After patting their noggins and filling their food bowls, I puttered into the greeting area and sat behind the historical desk. I checked reservations on the laptop and noticed a couple new names appeared. Last name Griddle. First names: Adam and Iris. *Hmm, I wonder if Joe knows them?*

P, B, T, and H trotted back and forth till I closed the computer and let them into the back yard. I filled a glass with apple juice and nibbled a handful of Granola. Just enough sustenance to tide me over till Grace's luncheon.

After letting the four-legged babies inside, I looked at my phone and noticed a missed call from Emily.

I returned her call, "Em, I'll be at Fenster Haus shortly--."

"Mom won't be there!" She blurted. "Can you believe she and Blake's mom are shopping in Greenville?"

"Didn't Tilly know about the luncheon?"

"I thought she did, but apparently I forgot to tell her. Now look at what I've done." Emily gulped and then blubbered. "I've ruined everything."

"Calm down, Em. Everything's not lost. Maybe you can ask Blake to text his mom with the info. Hopefully she'll come up with an excuse to get Grace back here."

"That's brilliant. Bye."

* * *

I slid into my VW and cruised to Fenster Haus. Although the distance from the Inn and restaurant were virtually non-existent, the air-conditioner in my vehicle felt so much better than the sweltering humidity outdoors. I parked in a spot in front of Sweetness and Sweaters. Grace knew I visited that store quite often.

I popped inside the shop where Sendy stood ready and waiting. "Here you go, Rae. The gift is under the tissue paper. Hope Grace likes it."

"Me, too. She can be a little--."

"No need to explain. Now skedaddle. Party starts in 45 minutes."

"Why don't you come? You know you're invited."

"You know what? I will go. Business is kinda slow today." She plucked her purse from behind the counter, pulled her hairbrush from the bag, ran it through her mane, and followed me out the door. "Oops, forgot to flip the sign to CLOSED."

The parking lot in front of Fenster Haus was practically empty. All the ladies took the stealth plan to heart. Carpool, walk, or park discreetly.

As Sendy and I entered the beautiful greenhouse, Emily scuttled toward me in desperation. "Rae, Tilly hasn't answered Blake's text. I'm horrified."

My mind raced. "Where's Natalie?"

Emily pointed to the community table. "She's over there, but what can she do?"

"Natalie is full of wisdom. She might have an idea."

I maneuvered around the tables and reached my Bitty's Buns' friend. "Natalie. We're in panic mode."

"Why?"

"Grace isn't here."

"She'll be here in ten minutes. Tilly and I schemed and plotted to keep Grace out of Hope this morning because we both know how nosy she can be. No worries. They're returning for a quiet lunch for the two soon-to-be grandmas. Or at least that's what Tilly told your mom-in-law." She grinned at Emily. "Also known as your mother."

Emily sank into a nearby chair and pretended to fan herself with a cloth napkin. "Well, I swanny!"

The clanging bell startled everyone except Victoria who shook it from side to side. "Ladies, get to your seats. Grace and Tilly just parked out front. Hurry up!"

All the chairs around each table were filled with Hope-ite ladies. Not a peep from anyone. Until the French door opened and in walked the guest of honor. "Surprise!" We all yelled.

I'd never seen Grace blubber and bawl like she did at that moment. Emily shifted out of her chair and swiveled around tables to hug her mother.

Victoria shook the bell again. "Welcome Ladies and gentle--."

"There are no gentlemen." Sendy's sister, Sea, interrupted. "Just us girls!"

Everyone roared with laughter as Shelly guided Grace to her reserved seat. Our Buds and Blooms' owner, Fran, stood behind my mom-in-law and placed a flowered garland crown on her head. "You are hereby, and forever more, dubbed Gladiolus."

The senior Mrs. Byer touched her crown, pulled a mirror from her purse, and giggled like a schoolgirl. "I declare!"

Fran stepped behind her own chair. "Grace, the gladiolus flower symbolizes strength and integrity. We all thought a crown of them represented your fortitude and dedication to all things Hope. Whether it be the Historical Society, your family and friends, or the university, this is a time to celebrate you. Right, ladies?"

The room blossomed in applause and the afternoon flittered along. I slipped the bag from Sweetness and Sweaters into Grace's hand. We all stood in honor of Grace's dedication and teamwork with Lance. Although he was the person retiring, we knew she deserved recognition as they both stepped into another adventure.

Grace glanced at the tissue paper filled gift bag. "What's this?"

Sendy giggled, "Open it and find out."

Charms spelling the words, Faith, Hope, and Love dangled from a silver bracelet and jingled on the senior Mrs. Byer's wrist. "I love it and I love y'all. I swanny, Ladies. I'm speechless."

We all clapped, hugged her neck, then dawdled to our cars with full bellies and goosebump memories.

Now we ask you, brothers and sisters to
acknowledge those who work hard among
you... 1 Thessalonians 5:12

Chapter 12

The scent of waffles and bacon lured me into the kitchen. Of course, four gargantuan hounds paraded behind me. "Molly, it smells absolutely wonderful."

"You seem to be over morning sickness. That's always a good thing." She filled a glass pitcher with warm syrup.

"I'm feeling much better." I poured myself a glass of milk. "Why are you cooking this deliciousness? Guests don't arrive till tomorrow."

"I'm always cooking at the restaurant and here for guests. I wanted to make breakfast especially for you."

"Me?"

"Yes, dear, you and the babies." She set a placemat on the island. "Now sit and enjoy."

"Not unless you join me." I pulled another placemat from the drawer and placed it next to mine.

We filled our plates with Belgian waffles, strawberries, and crispy bacon, then Molly prayed over our meal. "Lord, we praise You and love You. Thank You for this food, friendship, and these sweet babies." She patted my tummy.

I bit into the melt-in-your mouth waffle and crunched a piece of bacon. "This is scrumpdiliumpshis."

"What in the world are you saying, girl?"

"It's beyond scrumptious!"

"You're so silly. Now eat, dear. Gotta keep up your strength." She blew on her hot coffee then took a drink, "Rae, I'm having surgery next month and won't be 100 percent for a while."

"Molly, what's happening? How can I help? Don't worry about being at work." I slid off the stool and hugged her neck.

"It's a female thing. I've been needing this procedure for months. Sorry to desert you."

"Please don't feel that way. Just let me know what you, Henry, and the girls need, and Joe and I will do it."

"I have an idea but please don't feel any obligation to go along with it." She fiddled with a rogue strand of her hair. "Kelly would love to be the temporary chef while I'm recovering. She's been my Sous-chef since forever and knows your kitchen like its her own. I understand if that won't work."

"Molly, you don't have to convince me. I love you like a sister and trust your judgement completely. Kelly can definitely be our chef while you get better, but who's going to help Henry at the restaurant?"

"Oh, my hubby and I have everything under control. Sidney will help when she's not busy at Peaches and Cream. We are all in complete agreement. No worries at all." She rinsed our dishes and I placed them in the dishwasher. "Is it a go?"

"Absolutely!" Tears formed.

"No tears, dear. Now how many reservations are there for tomorrow? Do I know any of them?"

Anyone who is hungry should eat something at home... 1 Corinthians 11:34

Chapter 13

Joe shoved open the doors to the Inn. "Honey, I'm home!" He mumbled something about WD 40 to fix the squeaky doors.

I jumped at the sound of his grand entrance. "I'm in here." I shoved the chair under the desk and sauntered into his waiting arms. "Hey, soon-to-be Head of the University of South Carolina at Hope." Kisses.

"Come here, soon-to-be wife of the Head of the University of South Carolina at Hope."

I ducked out of his embrace and placed my hand on my hip. "What about the title, Inn at Hope owner? Doesn't that count for anything?" I flipped my hair in jest.

The back door screen slammed shut and our canines plowed into the entryway. Joe looked as bewildered as me.

Who let the dogs inside?

Uncle Quinn yelled. "Where are you two? The dogs wanted in." He removed his cowboy hat and scratched his forehead as he clomped into the foyer. "Didn't know you were down here. Thought you were upstairs."

Joe hung his backpack on a nearby hook, "Hey, Uncle Q. How can I help?"

I returned to the desk and opened the laptop. "Hi, Uncle Quinn. Are you and Sendy okay? Need anything?"

He shuffled near the antique desk, pulled up a chair, sat down, and fumbled with his well-worn hat. "There's trouble with Earnest and his team. They want the splash pad closer to the corral. That's not good."

Joe pushed a chair next to his. "When did you talk to Earnest? What did he say?"

"I haven't talked to him. I don't think he's qualified to work on that project."

A knock on the front door to the Inn surprised me. "I'll get that." The guys didn't budge.

I pulled the door open. "Come on in Earnest." I tried to say his name loud enough so my hubby and uncle could hear. "Joseph William Byer and Uncle Quinn, Mr. Timble is here."

With that, Joe and Uncle Q stood quickly and turned toward Earnest Timble. My hubby shook the contractor's hand and Uncle Quinn stiffened his gaze.

I slipped into a nearby chair.

Joe motioned for Earnest to have a seat. "Glad you're here. Anything on your mind?"

"Yes. I've gotta be honest." He looked at Uncle Q. "I think there's been some tension and I'm not sure why."

Our cowboy uncle interjected. "I feel the same. You're sneaking into my territory with that splash thing."

"Didn't you look at the recent blueprint? We've moved the splash pad farther from the corral or whatever it's called. One of my workers knows a thing or two about horses and said we were too close to the horse stuff."

"When did y'all change it?" Quinn put his hat back on his head. "I never heard about it."

Earnest leaned forward in his chair. "Quinn, we sent you an e-mail day before yesterday with all the information. I assumed you saw it."

"Nope. I don't check e-mail hardly ever. I like doing things the old-fashioned way. Man to man. I'd rather see where you've decided to put the splash thing in person."

Joe, Quinn, and Earnest strode toward the front doors. My hubby's eyes linked with mine. "Rae, I'm going with them. I think we've cleared up this mess." He punched Q and Earnest on their forearms. "Right fellas?"

No comment.

* * *

When my professor returned home, we sipped mugs of warm milk, nibbled chocolate chip cookies, and started a movie. Before the title appeared, I turned toward Joe. "Hunk, I'm so glad everything's settled with Uncle Q and Earnest." I chuckled.

"It's not settled. Uncle Q said he's not leaving Hope, barring anything important happening in Texas, until the splash pad is completed." He paused the movie.

"That man is as stubborn as a mule." I popped the last piece of cookie into my mouth.

"Ya know what? He's probably delivered a mule or two."

We roared with laughter and started the movie.

I snuggled into the crook of my hubby's arm. "You know what professor?" I sipped my milk. "Let's include Quinn in the decision making about other things not just the horses. What do ya think?" I winked.

"Wife of mine. I agree. Now let's start the movie."

* * *

After positioning a pillow under my side to help support my expanding middle, I squirmed to get comfortable in bed. "Joe, do you know the Griddles? They're arriving tomorrow with the rest of the folks for your dad's retirement."

Joe moved Buddy's paw from the middle of his back. "The Griddles? I've never heard of them." He plumped a couple pillows and rested his head. "Do they make pancakes on their griddle?"

I attempted to sit up and decided not to. Otherwise, Puff's might take more bed space. "Shame on you. People could say we buy everything with the name Byer."

"You don't like the last name?" He patted my tummy.

"I love it." Smooch.

Sleep overtook the Joe Byer domain. The four pony sized hounds nestled on our king-sized bed and snored in tandem. The babies and I snuggled on top of the duvet with the ceiling fan spinning. Pregnancy hormones.

A hot-tempered person stirs up conflict, but the
one who is patient calms a quarrel.
Proverbs 15:18

Chapter 14

I removed the plastic covering from Joe's suit, then carefully placed his burgundy and black striped tie on another hanger. His white cotton shirt pressed to perfection would hug my hubby's muscular physique tomorrow. I trembled a little at the thought of his new title. It never truly occurred to me until this moment that I'd be representing the university as Grace had done. Scary.

A paisley print maternity dress hung in my closet area. I stood back and glanced from my dress to Joe's promotion attire. *Paisley dress and Joe's striped tie?* I need Lauren's fashion advice. I'd no sooner thought of my dear friend, than a text from her appeared.

Lauren: I'm attending retirement!

Me: You can lv Wyoming??

Lauren: Mick said to go. I'm glad

Me: I'm thrilled. When do you arrive?!!!

Lauren: Look out your back door

I trotted downstairs as the dogs led the way. Lauren threw open the door, and hugged my neck, until Heidi whimpered and pranced for her attention. She bent down and hugged her awaiting puppy.

"I thought you needed to be in Wyoming to support Mick."

"He and his folks are regrouping and trying to get legal paperwork together. I'll fly back the day after the retirement. But for now, I'm here! Plus, I'm representing his grandma." She slid out of her shoes and plopped them on the floor of the mudroom. "I'll never get used to this globby red clay."

"Who cares about the dirt. What about his grandma?"

"I believe you have two guests arriving today?"

"You silly girl, all the cottages are reserved."

"With the last name Griddle?"

"How'd you know?"

"Adam and Iris?"

"Yes." I tried to place my hand on my hip but opted for my tummy. "How do you know them?"

Lauren strolled into the kitchen and pulled out two stools. "Here sister of mine." She motioned toward one of the stools. "Sit. I'll explain the details while I get us some juice." She opened the fridge.

"You're my guest, I'll serve you."

"Are you kidding me? I probably know this kitchen better than you do."

"You're right!" I sniggled. "Now talk while you serve me, please." I put my elbows on the island.

She maneuvered through the kitchen with ease. "Remember I told you Mick's grandma was Alana G. Treavor?"

"Yes."

"The G. stands for Griddle." She poured the juice into vintage glasses. "Iris and Adam are Mick's aunt and uncle. Adam is Grandma Alana's brother. He and Iris lived in Hope for years then moved to Beaufort, South Carolina. They're quite elderly and can't travel to Wyoming for the funeral but wanted to come to the retirement. So, Mick's mom and dad got them airline tickets. It's a very short flight from Beaufort to Spartanburg." She drank a little juice. "His folks asked if I'd help navigate my new relatives around town."

"That's wonderful. But I still need more details. Do they know the Byers?"

"They knew Joe's grandparents." She drank the last drop of her apple juice. "Adam and Iris Griddle donated money to build the dormitory at the university here in Hope."

"Really? I asked Joe if he recognized the name, but he didn't."

"Lance and Grace do. Mick didn't know anything about their connection with the university until his dad shared that info with him while tending to Grandma Alana's paperwork. She had a newspaper clipping of Adam and Iris in front of the dormitory." Lauren placed her glass in the sink.

"That kinda explains why Joe didn't know the name."

I stepped off the stool and carefully added my empty glass next to Lauren's. "I can't wait to meet the Griddles. Such a sweet connection with Hope and the Inn." I wiped the countertop. "Let's get you upstairs and settled into the guest room. By the way, where is the dormitory?"

"You know the big building on your new property?" She grinned. "Old dorms."

"You're kidding me! I'd better let Joe and Uncle Quinn know." I pushed the stools under the island. "But first things first, let's go upstairs to the guest room."

"No need, Sis. Mom and Daddy will be devastated if I don't stay with them. Honestly, it'd be easier if I stayed here so I can be on call for the Griddles since they're staying in a cottage." She cringed. "If you don't mind, may I put your guest room on hold?"

"Of course!"

The dogs led the parade upstairs with Lauren and me following close behind. "Make yourself at home while I call Joe with the news."

"Thanks for letting me stay--."

My phone buzzed. "It's Joe!" I slipped into a living room chair.

"Rae, you'll never guess what I found out." He didn't wait for an answer. "The old building used to be dormitories for the university." He took a deep breath.

"Oh, really?" I giggled.

"You found out?"

"Uh-huh."

"How? Did you talk to Mick? He told me about fifteen minutes ago."

"No. I'll give you three guesses and the first two don't count."

"Oh, Mrs. Byer you are a comedian." He groaned. "Mick told me Lauren's at the Inn and I'll bet that's how you found out."

"You should be a detective, Mr. Byer."

"Don't try to schmooze me, Wife. I'll contact Dr. Duntworth and Mr. Dells, unless you already have."

"No, I haven't." I laughed. "By the way, how about Uncle Quinn?"

"Bet he already knows."

"I wouldn't be surprised if your mother sent out an e-mail with every tidbit of the news."

We both roared with laughter and spurted. "Small town!" Call ended.

I slid my phone into my pocket and motioned to Lauren. "Please follow me, I need your fashion expertise."

"Maternity couture isn't in my wheelhouse, but I'll give it a try. What's the dilemma?"

"Come see."

She sauntered into my closet and pointed to the paisley print. "Pretty, but definitely not for a retirement. Especially when you'll be standing with Joe." She scanned through my dressy clothing. "You need something new." She closed the door. "Sweetness and Sweaters, here we come."

And now, dear lady, I am not writing you a new
command but one we have had from the
beginning. I ask that we love one another.
2 John 1:5

Chapter 15

The bell above the door at Sweetness and Sweaters jingled. Sendy stepped from behind the counter. "It's so good to see you newlywed girls. You both look radiant."

I giggled. "Sendy, what do you mean? You're a newlywed, too."

"Guess you're right. I love being married." She blushed then nodded at Lauren. "I heard your honeymoon is on hold, dear. I'm so sorry to hear about Grandma Treavor. It's precious that you're here for the retirement and related to the Griddles."

I started to ask how she knew but there was no need.

Sendy snatched a couple dresses from the rack then pulled a few from the back of the store. "Try these, Rae. I think you'll like the new line. You can wear them even after you have the babies." She smiled at Lauren. "Something new for you, Mrs. Treavor?"

Lauren grinned. "Definitely not maternity--."

Lauren's mom, Betty, entered the store through the back door and stopped in her tracks. "Baby girl, I heard you say maternity! Are you expecting? Am I going to be a grandma?" Betty reached for Lauren and hugged her neck. "Is it true?"

"No, mother, it's not true at all. You didn't hear everything I said." Betty slumped into Lauren's arms. "Mom, you'll be one of the first to know when Mick and I decide to add a child or two to our family."

"Well, okay, sweet daughter." She kissed Lauren's cheek. "The guest room at home is ready and waiting. You'll be the first to use it." She fluttered. "Will you join Daddy and me for dinner tonight?" She palmed her forehead. "Oh, my goodness, I'm smothering you. I forgot you're a married woman now. Come to think of it, you and Rae need time to visit." She waved to us. "Y'all have fun. Tata, girls."

"Lauren, I love your mom." I slipped into one of the dressing rooms and heard the door open to the room next to mine.

My sister tapped lightly on the wall. "Rae," she whispered. "I can't believe my mom thought I was pregnant. Do I look like I've put on a few pounds?"

I responded with a text.

Me: You're slim as ever.

Lauren: You sure?

Me: Thumbs up emoji

* * *

Lauren and I left with our purchases, then stepped a few paces behind Sendy's place to an adorable shop that literally housed almost anything from A to Z. Hence the name, Angels to Zithers.

Sea stood outside her shop and polished the brass doorknob. She pointed to the bags that Lauren and I carried. "I see you two have been to my sister's store. She always has the cutest clothes." Sea put down her cloth. "Lauren, I'm so sorry to hear about Mick's grandma and surprised to see you. I thought you were in Wyoming."

"I flew back for the retirement ceremony."

"Your in-laws are so glad you married Mick."

"Thank you, Sea. I appreciate that."

"Well, follow me, girls. I have a few new items y'all might be interested in." She opened the door, and Lauren and I stepped inside the luxurious mercantile.

Sea handed us vintage glasses filled with lemonade. "Looks like you could use a little refreshment."

I emptied my glass in two gulps. Not very ladylike, I might add, but thirst trumped etiquette. "Sea, how is Midnight adjusting at Izzy and Grady's?"

"That sweet cat is a perfect match for my daughter and son-in-love. The children are thrilled and never give the poor thing a moment's rest. They Facetime with Doris so she can see her precious Midnight. It's quite emotional, but she knows her kitty is loved." Sea refilled my drink. "The kiddos are settled in Sumter, South Carolina and rented a house off base. I can't wait to visit them when they give the okay. Boundaries, ya know."

The bell to Angels to Zithers ding-a-linged and in walked Emily. "Hey, Sea." She spotted the lemonade pitcher and poured herself a glass. "This is just what I need. I'm parched and hot as blazes. Just look at me. Swollen feet and hair that's as scraggly as ever. I'm getting it cut."

I handed her a tissue packet. "Here, Sis, this might help."

Lauren shuffled through her trendy purse and pulled out a hairclip. "You can have this, Emily. I have a bazillion of them."

"You gals spoil me." She set her glass down, twisted her hair into a French twist, and added the clip from Lauren. "That's so much better."

Sea refilled her glass. "Emily Wayne. You are radiant. Stop focusing on how you look. You're gorgeous and will have a beautiful baby. Cherish this time, dear. Not every lady has the opportunity to incubate a baby under her heart." She hugged my sister-in-law then nodded to the three of us. "I'll be in the back unpacking a couple boxes. Lauren, you must start shopping for your new home. Bet I have a few things you and Mick might like." She grinned. "Love ya, gals."

* * *

After visiting, strolling through the store, and weaving this way and that between exquisite items, Emily headed home in her Mini.

Lauren and I ambled into Bitty's Buns for a snack. Natalie escorted us to the back of the bakery. "I know you girls sometimes sit up front near the windows, but I thought you might like a little privacy to catch up on best friend stuff. What can I get y'all?"

Lauren didn't hesitate. "Banana cream pie and a cup of Hopes Rae, please."

Natalie winked at me. "What are you craving today, little lady? Pickles and ice cream?"

"Oh, you know me too well, Miss Natalie. Pickles, ice cream, and sardines with hot sauce."

She swatted at me with a cloth napkin. "Guess I deserved that after my sarcasm!"

"Coconut cream pie with a glass of cold milk. Water too, please."

She squinched her nose as if to squelch a laugh. "Want two pieces of pie since you have two babies to feed?"

This time I swatted at her with my cloth napkin.

My dear sister and I chitter chattered. "I'm so glad you're in town, Lauren."

"Do you need help getting ready for the massive arrival of cottage occupants?" She flung her straight, raven-colored mane over her shoulder.

"You've already helped me with my dress choice."

"Piece of cake."

Each of us should please our neighbors for their good, to build them up. Romans 15:2

Chapter 16

A serpentine line formed from the check-in desk and out the front doors of the Inn. Voices wove together as family and friends greeted each other and babbled non-stop while waiting for their cottage assignments. Joe and I hired Kramer to help with luggage. Fran and George's son, Clark, helped keep the dogs occupied in the back yard. Sidney and Hannah offered lemonade and sweet tea in clear plastic cups on the front porch. Of course, Joe and I tended to the needs of these special guests. Most of whom I'd never met.

Joe sat at the antique desk and motioned at the next person in line. "Welcome. Glad you're here."

"It's good to see you again, young man." The elderly gentleman reached across the desk to shake Joe's hand. "It's been a long time."

Joe stood and reciprocated. "Hello, sir."

In a nanosecond, Grace pushed through the line to where the man stood. "Adam, it's so good to see you. I'm so sorry about your sister, Alana." She scanned the foyer. "Where is Iris?"

"Thank you. Alana and I said our 'see you laters' a few months ago over the phone. I know she's in heaven and that gives me peace." Adam Griddle leaned on his cane. "Iris is sitting in my niece's car."

"Your niece's car?"

Lauren scooted next to Dr. Griddle. "Hi, Grace. Iris is waiting in my car."

My mother-in-law didn't skip a beat. "I swanny, Adam, I didn't even think about Lauren being related to you through marriage." She pushed her purse strap on her shoulder and patted his arm. "I'll assist you. Although you know this place like the back of your hand." She took his arm and looked at Joe. "Joseph, you remember Dr. Griddle, don't you, dear?" She didn't give him time to answer. "He was in charge of the university even before your dad had tenure."

Dr. Griddle threw his head back and chortled. "My goodness, Grace, the boy was a toddler. The only reason I recognized him is because of the Christmas cards you sent. There's no way he remembers me." He shifted his cane to his other hand and glanced at my mom-in-law. "Great seeing you. Guess I'd better get settled in."

"Just a sec, Lance and I are going to Molly's Restaurant for dinner at six. It would be wonderful if you and Iris joined us." Grace blew a corkscrew-shaped curl from her forehead. "Special is meatloaf with sides."

Adam shuffled toward the front doors then paused. "Sounds like old times when we all raced to that restaurant for staff lunches. It was named something different back then. You know what? Iris and I'll be there. Six, sharp."

Grace beamed, scampered toward the front doors, and announced, "Hope to see everybody at Molly's tonight for the special." She left and trotted to Lauren's car to speak with Iris.

I threaded around other guests toward Lauren's uncle. "If you follow me, sir, Kramer will help with your luggage."

Dr. Griddle leaned on his cane and cleared his throat. "You and Joe have really transformed this building. I'm impressed." He drew a handkerchief from his pocket and wiped beads of perspiration from his forehead. "Wish I could see the changes upstairs, but as you can see for yourself," his eyes focused on his cane, "stairs aren't my friend anymore."

"You know what? I'll take photos and if you don't mind, I'll send them to you and Mrs. Griddle."

"We'd love it. I noticed y'all have a golf cart out front. I think I'll hop on it." He pointed at his cane. "Maybe I'll forgo hopping and cautiously climb onto the contraption." He grinned at Lauren. "Iris isn't as mobile as I am. Please drive her to the cottage, niece." His shoulders crackled a bit as he looked over his shoulder. "Joe, you'll do a great job." He waved and crept out the doors at a snail's pace.

***

Our guests settled in their cottages. The Inn at Hope filled to the brim. A block of rooms at a hotel in Greenville were reserved for other retirement ceremony attendees. Joe, the dogs, and I meandered upstairs to our domain.

"Rae, sit down on the sofa, Honey. Your legs and feet must be killing you. Let me give them a rub down." He sat at one end of the couch.

I didn't need any more convincing and stretched out on the sofa. "Thanks, Joseph."

***

Joe gently nudged my shoulder. "Wake up, Beautiful. It's supper time."

I realized I'd fallen asleep on the sofa, then reached up and hugged his neck. "I can't believe I've slept this long. We need to deliver the snack bags to the cottages."

"No, we don't. Natalie delivered them. She texted me after she took them to each cottage. She knew if she offered, we'd refuse."

"She's such a gift to us, Joe."

"She sure is--."

My phone buzzed. "It's a text from Lauren."

"Go ahead and read it." He smiled that crooked grin of his and helped me up from the sofa.

I read the text out loud.

Lauren: Sitting in usual booth at Molly's. Emily and Blake are too.

I yawned, then looked at my hubby. "Wanna go?"

"Sure."

Me: Be there in a few. Smiley emoji

"Beautiful, tonight's the meatloaf special."

"I look like I've eaten a few of those specials with a belly like this." I rubbed my tummy.

"I love that belly."

I made a beeline for the bathroom, freshened up, then moseyed downstairs with Joe.

We fed and watered our mongrels, let them outside to do their business, and back in to enjoy the comforts of air conditioning.

* * *

I chuckled at the sound of Molly's greeting as we entered the restaurant. "Rae and Joe, your reserved seats are over there." She pointed to our usual booth. "Excuse me, everyone. The university athletic teams will serve each booth and table and clean up after supper this evening. Our honorary guests, Dr. and Mrs. Griddle, Lance and Grace Byer, Ike Wood, and Joe and Rae, and anyone else I unintentionally forgot, will be served first." She waved a flag with the Gamecock logo then proceeded to jab it into a vase of Jasmine—the state flower.

Uncle Quinn chortled. "Since I'm Grace's brother, can I be first, too?"

Sendy rolled her eyes and tugged at his shirt sleeve. Everyone roared with laughter.

Except Grace. She hid her head in her hands then shook her finger at her little brother. "Just for that, Quirky Quinn, you'll be last." She folded her arms in front of her and attempted to curtail a grin. No use in trying. She roared along with the crowd.

A line of cheerleaders and athletes formed outside the kitchen and delivered our food in unison.

The chatter in the room filtered out the sound of background music until Mayor Sounds cradled a microphone to his mouth. "Ladies and gentlemen, let's give a round of applause for the Athletic Department." Applause erupted from every corner of the dining area. "Thanks for coming tonight. Just a reminder that tomorrow is Lance Byer's retirement, and Joe will fill his shoes. See you in the morning."

Victoria, the mayor's wife, and parliamentarian for the Historical Society, tapped her hubby's shoulder. "May I have the mic?" She didn't wait for him to answer and slid it from his clutches. "Thanks, dear." She placed the device to her mouth. "Don't forget. Tomorrow is Grace's retirement, too." The ladies of Hope stood, whooped, and hollered. "Remember, Rae will need our support, too, ladies." Applause.

I sat on the bench seat between Lauren and Joe, and Lauren leaned in my direction. "See, Rae, you'll have lots of help. You'll do great, Sis."

I cringed. "Hope you're right."

"I'm right here for you."

Emily added, "I'm here for you, too, Rae. You're not alone." She smiled at Lauren. "Rae and I are here for you, too, girl. Once you're a part of the Historical Society you'll need a shoulder to cry on." She raked strands of hair behind her ear. "Lauren, I'm just kidding about the crying part. But I'm serious about Rae and me being available." She looked at me. "Right sis-in-law?"

"Right. We're in this together. I love you both."

* * *

Home. Joe munched popcorn while watching a baseball game on TV with the dogs strewn across the living room sectional. Bathroom door closed. Me soaking in a warm bath, a mug of milk on the tiny table next to the tub, and soft music in the background. Heavenly.

My phone buzzed. I carefully slid it off the table and read a text from Lauren.

Lauren: I'll be at Inn 7:30 a.m. Rest well sister. Heart emoji

Me: Thank you! Love you!

* * *

I snuggled against my hubby's side and listened to Puffs and Buddy snoring at the foot of the bed. Trixie squinched between P and B. Heidi was staying the night with Lauren.

"Good night, Joseph. I love you," I whispered.

"Good night, Beautiful. I love you."

We melted into peace-filled sleep.

> *Do not forget to show hospitality to strangers,*
> *for by so doing some people have shown*
> *hospitality to angels without knowing it.*
> *Hebrews 13:2*

Chapter 17

Joe and I awoke before dawn. "Rae, I'm so thankful for you. We make a great team, Beautiful." He held my hand and kissed it. "Who'd have ever thought I'd be able to follow in my dad's footsteps."

"Me." I kissed his lips. "I'm proud of you."

A rap on the door to our upstairs domain sent our fur babies into barking mode. Joe hopped out of bed, wrapped himself in his terry robe, and headed for the door as I made a beeline into the bathroom.

I heard Lauren's voice. "Hi Joe, I know it's early, but Molly made this delicious breakfast for you and Rae. I told her I'd deliver it to you."

I poked my head outside the bathroom door. "Thank you, Sis. You're the best. Stay and eat with us." I pulled my hair into a ponytail and scooted out the door into the living room.

Lauren placed the tray of food on a small table. "I got here earlier than I expected, and I've already eaten. I'll be downstairs helping Molly even though she has everything under control." She opened the door then looked our way. "Congratulations, you two. I'm so happy for you."

I scuttled toward her and hugged her waist. "I love you, Lauren. Thank you for being the bestest sister ever." My eyes misted.

"Rae, don't let those tears stain my dress." She winked and hugged me even tighter. "As your sister-in-law said, we're in this together." She strutted toward the door and glanced back. "By the way, I got a text from Grace late last night. She said I'll be up for a vote into the Historical Society at the next meeting." She cringed then winked. "I'll be downstairs if you need anything."

* * *

I looked at my prince charming in his three-piece suit. "Professor, you look so handsome." I reached up to straighten his burgundy and black tie and couldn't resist that crooked grin of his. "Lean down here, Hunk." I plastered a kiss of all kisses on his lips then pulled from his embrace.

My hubby's flushed face almost looked like the burgundy color on his tie. "You've made my day." He grinned.

"Mine, too." I wound my hair into a side bun, added a love knot pearl barrette, and slipped into my new dress. My silhouette in the full-length bathroom mirror made me chuckle. "Yes, little ones. We're off on a new adventure today."

Joe stood in the doorframe. "Who ya talking to, Mrs. Byer?"

"Our babies."

"Thought so." He bent down, tapped my bulging baby bundle, and whispered, "We're in this together, little ones." He kissed my tangerine flavored lips. "I love you."

*Go through the camp and tell the people, 'Get
your provisions ready… Joshua 1:11*

Chapter 18

Joe parked his clunky truck in a reserved spot in front of the university. He pointed out the window at the packed parking lot and squiggled his brows, "My detective skills say it's time to go inside."

"Professor, your investigative skills are so amazing." I fluttered my eyelashes at him then paused as butterflies of anxiety fluttered in my stomach. I slid across the bench seat as modestly as I could. Then Joe helped me exit the truck. My open-toed heels required navigational skills and hubby assistance.

We strolled hand in hand into the University of South Carolina at Hope. I halted inside the door. "Joe, I'm nervous."

"Nervous--?"

"Petrified is probably a better description."

Dean Ike Wood stood at the entryway to the auditorium. His toothy smile caused me to grin. "Rae and Joe, I get to be your escort to your reserved seats. I'm honored the staff chose me." He held onto his walker. "Come follow me."

I'd never seen Ike use a walker. We sauntered after him to our chairs.

Ike sat in the front row next to me. "Mr. Ike, I can't think of anyone I'd rather have escort Joe and me." I patted his frail arm. "Love you."

"I'm honored. I love you and Joe, too. You always make Penny and me feel special."

I whispered. "Where's Penny?"

"She's sitting with Lauren."

* * *

The event began with the pledge of allegiance and national anthem. Lance spoke with confidence and certainty that his decision to retire was God's will. "Thank y'all for coming. Grace and I are so grateful..." His emotional speech brought tears and laughter to all of us.

I'd never heard my father-in-law speak so profoundly.

He motioned for Grace to join him on the platform. "In conclusion, I want to thank my bride for being at my side all these years." He kissed her cheek. "It's hard to believe the time has passed this quickly."

Standing ovation. The Historical Society ladies and university alumni stood on the stage with Grace and Lance for a photo. Then Lance kissed Grace's cheek and proceeded to sit in his reserved seat on the front row.

Grace started to follow Lance until Emily took her hand and stood next to her. I held onto Emily's hand. All the ladies in the auditorium held hands and formed a circle around the room. Victoria spoke to Grace and the audience. "We are here to honor Grace Byer with a small gift. Anne, will you get that for our esteemed friend?"

Anne picked up a wrapped box off a nearby chair. "Grace, we love you and hope you like this."

"Ladies, you've already given me this beautiful bracelet which I absolutely love." She jingled her charms then focused on her newest gift. She meticulously untaped the paper from the outside of the box, removed the burgundy tissue paper, and held an album to her chest. "Well, I swanny. This is..." She gulped and whimpered as she fumbled through the pages. "The time y'all took to make this for me... I'm speechless." She held the present above her head for all to see. "Look at what it says on the cover of the photo album. *Grateful for Grace, With love, the University of South Carolina and all the Ladies of Hope.*"

The event ended with hugs, promises to keep in touch, and sincere best wishes to the newly retired Byers. The residents formed a line down Beaufort Street and around the lake so we could wave to Grace and Lance as they drove home. However, the two of them surprised us. They drove slowly down the main street, passed a few houses in the circle, and didn't even pause at Dean and Mrs. Lance Byer's abode. Instead, Lance gunned the engine on his Ford, the two of them waved to everyone, and off they went.

Joe waved and applauded his folks. "Rae, guess where they're going?"

"I don't have a clue!"

Emily tugged at Joe's sleeve. "How do you know where they're going, and I don't?" She folded her arms across her tiny baby bump.

Joe looked at Em and me. "Dad told me when you two were standing in a circle with all the other ladies. Mom didn't have a clue until they left the ceremony."

Emily fixed her messy bun. "Well, daddy could have told me too."

I noticed Blake whisper in Emily's ear and her countenance softened. "Where are they going?"

Joe grinned. "I'm not telling."

"Big Bro, you'd better tell me." She stood toe-to-toe with Joe, and the two of them teased like only brothers and sisters can do.

Their sense of humor always made me laugh. *I hope our children do the same someday.*

Joe patted the top of her head. "Okay, guess I'll give in. Dad made hotel reservations across the states in places he and Mom have only dreamed about. They're not sure when they'll get home."

Emily's eyes bulged, "You mean they might not be here to meet their grandbaby?"

Blake took her hands in his. "Em, you know without a shadow of a doubt your mom wouldn't miss the baby's birth. She and my mom already have everything planned for delivery day. No worries, Hon."

Emily cradled against his side as they strolled towards Bitty's Buns. "I love you, Blakey."

Joe and I climbed into his truck. "Joe, this has been such a wonderful time. The ceremony was beautiful." I held tightly to his right hand as he navigated the brick street toward the Inn.

"It really was a great event. I'm glad Dad surprised Mom. You know how hard it is to surprise her!"

"I do!"

Joe parked in front of our abode.

"Professor, would you mind if I text Lauren? She leaves tomorrow."

"Nope."

I sent a text:

Me: Lauren, are you busy?

Lauren: I've taken Griddles to their cottage. Want to do something?

I waited to text her. "Joe, do we have any plans?"

"Why don't you and Lauren go to lunch. I've got stuff to do before I start the new job."

I smooched those tempting lips of his. Then sent Lauren another message.

Me: Lunch at Fenster Haus?

Lauren: Perfect. I'm at my folks

Me: I'll pick you up in 30 min

Lauren: Thumbs up

So you too should be glad and rejoice with me.
Philippians 2:18

Chapter 19

Puffs, Buddy, and Trixie wiggled and jiggled when we arrived home. I loved kissing those gargantuan noses and fluffing their ears. When I let them out the back door, they zoomed outside. *I wonder if they miss Midnight. I miss her and Miss Doris.*

I traipsed upstairs to change and saw Joe sitting on the top step. "You okay, Handsome?"

"Guess I'm a little emotional about the retirement. It's a neat thing. But it also says my folks are getting a lot older. I know that's the way things are supposed to happen." He patted the spot on the step next to him. "I can't complain, though, can I? You lost your folks at such a young age. I'm so sorry about that." He raked his fingers through his hair.

"Joseph William Byer, you have such a tender heart. I look at the freedom your folks have right now and am so happy for them. I'll bet your dad is so relieved that you're taking his position and that makes everything easier for him." I kissed his nose. "Am I right? Or am I right?"

He kissed my lips. "You're right, Mrs. Joseph Byer. You'll be such an asset to the University of South Carolina at Hope. I can't wait for this new beginning."

* * *

Summer sun dappled through the trees and inside Fenster Haus. Blue hydrangeas, and azaleas nestled between the tree trunks.

Shelly Rodriguez guided Lauren and me to a table at the back of the restaurant. "Lauren, I'm so sorry to hear about Alana Treavor's passing. My grandparents knew her well."

Lauren slid into her chair. "Thank you, Shelly. How did your grandparents know her?"

She handed us our menus. "I'll tell you when I have more time. It's quite an emotional story." Her lips quivered. "Well, you gals, enjoy your meal." She winked at me. "You need to order extra, Rae. I hear you're expecting more than one."

I grinned from ear to ear and nodded.

Shelly swung around and glided toward guests at the front of the dining room.

I looked up from my menu then laid it on the table. "Lauren, the Historical Society ladies are in 7-C mode."

"I thought you said they're in plan 4-B mode because of Doris' hip surgery."

"We're all taking turns delivering protein snacks to her daughter, Hazel, since she is eating meals at the rehab center with her mother. Doris will be out of rehab soon and move to Kansas to live with Hazel and her family. So, plan 4-B will come to an end soon. We'll keep sending individual snail mail cards to encourage Doris. Since Grandma Griddle passed, you and Mick are our plan 7-C. I told Grace I'd check on you."

"Check on me? What do you mean?" She cocked her head.

"Plan 7-C makes sure you are doing okay. If you and Mick need any help with transportation, hotel, anything we will help--."

"Rae, that's nice of the ladies, but you know we are just fine. Grandma Griddle will be buried on her ranch next to Mick's grandpa. The only help we need is with Heidi, and you and Joe are watching our gargantuan pup for us. Thanks."

The server approached our table. "Hello ladies. May I take your order?"

We chose the same thing, and after nibbling on our hors d'oeuvre of artichoke dip and pita bites, our meal arrived. The aroma of roasted chicken, asparagus, twice baked potatoes, and yeast rolls floated through the air.

Lauren placed a cloth napkin in her lap, "I'll say grace." She bowed her head and so did I. "Lord, thank You for loving us and for creating the people who prepared this meal. Jesus, I especially thank You for creating my sister, Rae. Amen."

"Thank you for that beautiful prayer, Lauren. We are so blessed. Since the beginning of time, we've been there for each other. I'm so glad we are now, too." My eyes misted. "I guess Grace is right. My hormones are raging."

She patted my hand and laughed, "You have a tender heart, hormones or no hormones."

"Crazy girl. You always know what to say to stop me from whimpering." I smeared butter on my warm roll and took a mouth full.

"I need your listening ears, Sis. This is going to sound sorta weird since Mick and I just got married. It's something we talked about when we were dating."

I placed a small piece of roll on the bread plate. "Is everything okay? You're not sick or anything are you, Lauren?" I felt parallel lines form on my forehead.

She shook her head. "Oh no, it's nothing like that." She put her fork down. "We're so excited that you and Joe are expecting your sweet babies. I can't wait to be an aunt!"

"You'll be a great one."

"Mick and I want to adopt. Does that sound silly?" She slumped.

"Oh, dear sister, it sounds wonderful. Why would you ever think I'd think differently? Joe and I love you and Mick. Your children and ours will always be family. Just like you and me. We aren't biological sisters, but we are sisters. You know what I mean." I patted her hand.

"Yes, I do. You and I are sisters forever and ever." She pulled a tissue from her purse and wiped her nose. "I love you, Rae."

"I love you, too, Lauren."

We jibber jabbered until our dishes were practically clean.

Shelly strolled in our direction. "You girls, okay?"

I placed my fork on my plate, "We are, Shelly. Just sister stuff."

"I know exactly what you mean. When my sisters and I get together the tears flow. Mostly tears of joy." She swung around then turned back in our direction. "Tiramisu on the house for the two of you this evening. Seeing y'all makes me realize I need to call my big sis who lives in Wyoming."

I patted my nose with a tissue. "Thank you, Shelly. You're a blessing."

Lauren added, "And whenever you have time, I hope you'll let Rae and me know the connection our families have."

"I definitely will." Shelly turned and trekked to the front of the eatery.

Lauren finished her meal. "This was so delicious."

"Scrumdiliumpshus." I added.

We reminisced about the past and babbled about the future. When the tiramisu arrived, we thought we couldn't even take a nibble. Until one bite turned into two, and before we knew it, our porcelain dessert plates emptied.

* * *

I drove Lauren to her mom and dad's. "Rae, I'll see you in the morning when we pick up Iris and Adam. They're flying on a quick flight home to Beaufort the same time I fly to Wyoming."

"Do y'all need a ride to the airport?"

"No thanks, Mom and Dad are driving us. Thanks for keeping Heidi. Mick and I appreciate it so much. Keep me posted on the dorm research. Hope it's not historical. I'll see you soon, Sis." She squeezed my hand.

"I love you, Lauren. Remember plan 7-C. If you need any--."

"I know. If I need anything at all you'll be available. I love you little Historical Society member."

I sniggled. "You'll be one of 'us' before you know it, little soon-to-be society member."

She rolled her eyes, pulled herself out of the VW, and her long legs propelled her up the steps and onto the porch in no time at all. She waved from inside the door.

Oh yes, Sis, you'll be part of the group before you know it. We'll have a ball.

Dear friend, I pray that you may enjoy good health and that all may go well with you, even as your soul is getting along well. 3 John 1:2

Chapter 20

The Griddles checked out of the Inn. They promised they'd sort through old photos of the dormitory they had at home. Both Iris and Adam liked Joe's idea of including a little nostalgia into the design of the projected recreation building. After all, history was important to the residents of Hope. Especially my professor.

Uncle Quinn and Sendy informed us they didn't want breakfast this morning. They were our only guests for a few days, so Molly took the day off. I snatched a cranberry/orange scone off the glass covered plate on the counter. "Joseph, want something that'll stick to your ribs for breakfast?"

"Nah, but come here, Gorgeous. You're all I need." He slid his arms around my substantial middle, kissed my lips, and slow danced with me in the kitchen.

"My goodness, Mr. Byer, you are quite the schmoozer--."

"Uh-hum." Uncle Quinn cleared his throat and stood with arms folded.

My hubby and I dropped from each other's embrace.

"I let myself in the front doors. Sign says, OPEN. Need to talk to you, nephew." He tapped his cowboy boot on the floor and attempted to rake his fingers through his military haircut. "Sendy will be here in a sec."

I pointed at the coffee pot. "How about a cup, Uncle Quinn."

"No thanks."

Joe grabbed a napkin and wiped my Tangerine lip gloss from his lips. He added a single cup into the Keurig and brewed himself a strong cup of java. "How can I help you?"

Within seconds Sendy entered the kitchen. Her smile put me at ease. "Quinn, I see why your sister calls you Quirky and your grandchildren call you Papa Quirky. You look like a bear." She batted at him with a tissue.

He bellowed with laughter. "Come here you sweet thing." He reached for Sendy and wrapped her in a loving embrace, then gained his composure. "We'd like to treat you both to lunch. We know it's last minute, but we want to congratulate you on your new position at the university." He punched Joe's arm. "I'm proud of you, nephew."

Joe looked at me and I at him. "Sounds wonderful."

"Pick you up at noon. Sendy said we must eat somewhere that doesn't serve barbeque brisket because I always compare it with the Texas style. There's nothing better."

Sendy meandered my way. "This meal is to congratulate you too, precious Rae." She turned and strutted toward her hubby. "Quinn promised there'd be no shop talk during the meal."

Joe and I cracked up as we watched Q and Sendy walk out the front door. Quinn's fingers were crossed behind his back. He glanced over his shoulder and winked at the two of us.

"Joseph, I can't believe you're related to that man!"

"So are you." Crooked grin. "Okay, wife, we have three hours till lunch. I'm going to see what's happening with the four buildings. Let's talk to Uncle Quinn today about a town hall meeting for the locals."

"I agree with Sendy. No shop talk at lunch."

"You know that's not happening." He snickered. "I want input on classes we can offer in the spaces and any other suggestions Quinn, Sendy, and anyone else has."

I snatched my boots from the mud room. "Will you help me put on my boots?"

"Do you feel like tromping there?"

"Absolutely."

My Prince Charming helped slip them onto my feet. Just like glass slippers—well, sort of.

> *In that day each of you will invite your*
> *neighbor to sit under your vine and fig tree...*
> *Zechariah 3:10*

Chapter 21

Dr. Duntworth stood in the doorway to the first building. "Hey, you two, come inside. When you figure out what you want to use this for, I'll get students to build what you want. They need extra credit anyway." He removed his hardhat, pulled the infamous rag from his overall pocket, and wiped his perspiring dome. He stepped inside so Joe and I could enter.

I stood in complete amazement. "Dr. D, this is perfect. The original shiplap walls look rustic and…" I carefully rubbed my hand on the exposed boards. "Rich. They look even better than I thought they would."

Dr. Duntworth pointed to an area in the corner. "There's a water hookup over there. Maybe this could be used for art classes or some such thing. Mrs. D came by the other day and thought that might be a good idea. You might not know it, but my wife is a retired art teacher." He shoved the rag back into his pocket. "She knows you might have plans already."

I need to catalogue that information. Maybe she could teach classes.

Joe examined the double paned windows and the extraordinary workmanship. "Hold that thought, Dr. D. I need to send a text."

I whispered in Joe's ear. "A text?"

He murmured, "To Uncle Quinn. I want to find out if he likes the idea of a community meeting before I mention it to Dr. D."

"Great idea."

He sent the text.

Uncle Q: Agree

Joe showed me the response, then turned toward Dr. Duntworth. "We want to involve the local community in the plans. Uncle Quinn, Rae, and I can set up a town hall meeting."

"Yvette and I'll attend." We stepped outside and Dr. D locked the door to the building, "I have an idea for the smallest structure."

"What?"

"Restrooms." He wiped his forehead with the rag. "Wanna see the rest of the buildings?"

Joe and I chuckled then gave a thumbs up.

* * *

We traipsed home and Joe opened the back door. "Rae, let me help you with your boots. I'll wash that red dirt off them outside with the hose. You look a little flushed, Honey. Why don't you get some water?"

I kissed his cheek and held onto the rail as he slid the boots from my feet. "That sounds good, then I'll get a shower."

He set my boots on the top step. "Great idea."

I gulped a glass of water, then traipsed upstairs. The cool shower felt refreshing, and an oversized chartreuse terry towel felt so luxurious. I drew a brush through my tangled mane then proceeded to blow dry my hair and pull it in a ponytail. A melon-colored cotton dress with cap sleeves and white pea-sized buttons trailing halfway down the back fit me comfortably.

Joe trudged into the bathroom, "Rae, I took the dogs outside and on the way in I got a call from Mom." He kissed my neck. "By the way, you look gorgeous."

"Thank you, Handsome." I turned and hugged his waist. "Your mom? Everything okay?"

"She's fine. Believe it or not, she heard about the possibility of us scheduling a town hall meeting. She wants to be here when we do."

"She knows? Guess I shouldn't be surprised! If it's in a day or two, your dad's plans will go down the drain."

"I told her we'll give folks the option of participating in person or on the computer so there's no need to return."

"What did she say?"

"She didn't say a thing. I heard dad in the background. He blurted, 'Son, we're on our second honeymoon. Send the web connection, and we'll participate via the computer.' Then Mom added, 'Sounds like a great idea.' And they ended the call."

"That's fabulous!" I sniggled.

* * *

Uncle Quinn drove us to lunch in his truck toward the Fish Factory in a small town near Spartanburg. The mouthwatering flakey fish, tartar sauce, coleslaw, and hushpuppies were undeniably the best I'd ever tasted.

Joe took my hand in his. "Uncle Quinn and Sendy, we can't thank you enough for bringing us here. It's delicious."

Uncle Q gulped his sweet tea. "Aw, niece and nephew. This is a small thing Sendy and I can do for y'all. Now let's get down to business." He grinned.

Sendy glared at him. "Oh no you don't, tall Texan. No work talk. You promised."

"Well, Sugar, you didn't see me cross my fingers when I promised." He kissed her cheek.

"No sugar for you."

He slumped. "Well, okay I guess she wins. No shop talk."

Sendy giggled. "Okay, I give in. This might be the only opportunity the four of us can discuss the plan without the masses." She fluttered her eyelashes at her hubby. Sendy had that man wrapped around her little finger.

Joe laughed. "Now let's get started." He snatched his phone from his jeans pocket. "I'm making a list."

That's all Quinn needed to hear. He squared shoulders and put his elbows on the table, "First things first. Sendy and I aren't staying in South Carolina year round. Despite your mom's urgent request, we'll be in Texas half the year like we planned."

"I agree, Uncle Q. Mom's request is defunct. We have bigger fish to fry." Joe bantered.

Uncle Quinn almost tipped over on his teetering chair. "That's a good one, Joe, since we're eating fish!" His enormous grin turned into a solemn expression. "I can't take notes since I didn't bring a clip board or anything, and I don't have my phone."

Sendy pulled her cell from her purse. "Here, Sugar, use mine."

We brainstormed as the waiter refilled our glasses. We knew all the residents' suggestions were needed for the smaller structures and would eventually be needed for the large building.

I palmed my forehead with my hand. "You know what? Let's have the meeting on the land between the buildings. I know it might be hot, but if we meet about seven it should be bearable. What do y'all think?"

Sendy fluttered. "I think it's terrific. We can ask everyone to bring their own lawn chairs and tapas."

Quinn leaned as far back in his chair as possible without toppling the thing. "I know what lawn chairs are. But tapas? What's that?"

Sendy kissed his cheek. "You big lug, I love you to pieces." She leaned in closer to him. "Tapas are little hand-held snacks that can be hot or cold."

Quinn roared, "If they're snacks then call them snacks!"

Joe reached across the table and shook Q's hand. "I'm with you Unc!" He drank some of his tea. "I'll send a text to Mayor Sounds to make sure Monday night is available for a town meeting."

We all agreed.

Within minutes, Joe received confirmation from the Mayor that Monday evening at 7:00 was a go.

The fellas discussed items needed for the horses. Sendy and I ignored the two of them as we sent the informative e-mail to all the residents:

IMPORTANT TOWN HALL MEETING

What: Brainstorming about the new buildings. Come with suggestions for the name of our new recreation area.

When: Monday evening at 7:00 p.m.

Where: Land near the buildings*

Please bring lawn chairs and finger snacks to share.

*In case of rain, we'll meet at the Inn at Hope and fit as many folks as possible inside.

The entire afternoon melted into evening. We arrived home and Sendy and Quinn entered their cottage. Such a special family time.

* * *

Joe and I settled in early for the evening. Since Uncle Q and Sendy were our only guests, we knew they didn't need to be disturbed.

Joe fed and watered the hounds, started popcorn in our popper, and poured us glasses of apple juice. Of course, those crazy canines paraded up the steps behind Joe as the scent of buttery popcorn tempted their nostrils. With my hubby sitting next to me on the sectional and the dogs doing the best begging ever, I settled in the crook of Joe's arms. We munched and crunched in tandem to the music on the old record player. No TV tonight.

Better a dry crust with peace and quiet than a
house full of feasting, with strife. Proverbs 17:1

Chapter 22

I dragged myself from under the covers and stretched as far as my arms would reach. I heard Joe singing our song, *"Everything,"* from the bathroom and Puffs, Buddy, Trixie, and Heidi barked with every note.

I trudged into the restroom. "Joseph William Byer, if you're trying to wake me up, you've succeeded."

He slathered shaving cream on his face and cradled his razor in his hand. "Sorry, Honey. I couldn't resist singing our song. And neither could the dogs." Sheepish grin.

"Sure, you couldn't, Mr. Byer." I pulled my hair into a ponytail then watched him draw the razor over his morning beard. *Handsome man.* "Look at those silly pups. Have they gone outside yet?"

"I think they were waiting for you to wake up. I'll take them out, Beautiful."

"No need." I motioned to the dogs. "Come on you crazy fur babies. Follow me." I snatched my robe off the shiny hook on the bathroom door, stood on tiptoe, and kissed those tempting lips of my southern gentleman. "Let's go."

"Sure. I'll follow you anywhere." Joe dropped his razor in the sink.

"You know I'm talking to the dogs." I winked.

"A fella can hope, can't he?" He snatched the razor from the sink and proceeded to finish shaving.

The pups darted downstairs ahead of me and out the back door like they used to when Midnight teased them. Only this time, an orange feline perched on a low hanging pecan tree branch. "Better watch out. These humongous hounds are in pursuit." I traipsed down the back steps and into the yard. "That's enough, you four." The cat jumped from branch to branch, landed outside our fence, then scampered toward our new land.

Joe opened the back door. "What were they barking at?" He straightened his button-down collar.

"A cat. I'll bet it's the one we saw at the barn nursing her babies when Lauren and Mick got married. It was on that tree and ran off."

"Haha, maybe I need to get my catcher's mask and ball mitt out of the storage building. It came in handy with Midnight." He laughed.

"Silly guy." I rolled my eyes, slipped through the door, and into the kitchen. I took two bowls from the cupboard and filled them with granola. "Come on, Prof, breakfast is served." I opened the fridge, took out the milk, and poured it over the cereal.

Joe brought the pups inside, fed, and watered them. "I love your homecooked breakfasts, Sweetheart."

"You're in trouble now, Mister. Just for that I won't add a banana to your concoction." I sliced it into circles and added them to my bowl. Then discreetly sliced some for him, too.

He poured me a glass of apple juice then made himself a cup of coffee. "Let's pray, wife of mine."

Oh, how I love that man.

* * *

The church pews filled quickly. I chuckled to myself when I noticed no one sat in Grace and Dad Byer's spot. Not that it was reserved or anything. But in some ways, it was an unspoken sort of thing.

The sound of a baby's whimper drew my gaze to the left side of the sanctuary. Baby Daisy snuggled against Earnest's shoulder, while Collette removed a pacifier from a trendy baby bag. Collette caught my eye after she slipped the binky into Daisy's little rosebud mouth. She mouthed, "Good to see you."

I did the same then decided to slip out of the pew and head her way. "I'm so glad you stayed in Hope for the weekend."

Collette grinned. "We've traveled to Beaufort each weekend but decided not to this time. By the way, we love renting Lauren's home. It's perfect."

"Are y'all coming to Fenster Haus after the service?"

Earnest interjected, "Is it okay if we bring Daisy?" He handed her to Collette.

"Collette and Earnest, babies are allowed everywhere." I folded my arms in front of me and smiled. "They better let babies inside restaurants. I'm having two in the fall." I chuckled.

Collette laughed. The music started playing and she whispered. "I'm so excited for you and Joe." She spoke softly to Earnest. "Wanna go to lunch with the group?"

"Sure."

I excused myself and soft-stepped to the other side of the sanctuary. After explaining to Joe that the Timbles were joining everyone for lunch, we settled in for worship.

Until I felt a tap on my shoulder and heard Emily's voice. "Timbles okay? They usually go to Beaufort."

"They decided to stay in Hope this weekend and are joining us at Fenster Haus for lunch."

"Fantabulous."

* * *

The community table and smaller tables inside Fenster Haus were filled with Hope-ites. It was weird with Lauren and Mick gone and my in-laws absent.

Mayor Sounds tapped his water goblet. "Friends and family, let's return thanks." He cradled Victoria's hand in his. "Thank You, Lord, for loving us and for giving us this special place to relax and enjoy each other's company. Please be with our dear friends and owners, Shelly, Javier, and their children. Thank You, Jesus. Amen."

Victoria Sounds added, "Lord, please let the meeting tomorrow evening go wonderfully. Amen."

Everyone chitter-chattered about the buildings on our land. They shared ideas about the larger building becoming a recreation center. I scribbled a list of their suggestions on several napkins.

Lottie scampered in my direction. "Dear, if you'd like, I'll type those ideas on my computer this evening and send them to you through e-mail."

"Can you read my chicken scratch?" I showed her my list.

"Rae, if I have any questions, I'll text you. No need to be concerned, dear." She took the napkins from me and walked back to her chair. "Ladies and gentlemen, aren't we all super thankful that the possibility of a rec center even exists in this small town? Thank you, Quinn, Joe, and Rae!"

Church members and guests shouted, "Hear, hear!"

For where two or three gather in my name,
there am I with them. Matthew 18:20

Chapter 23

Joe opened the front doors to the Inn. My phone beeped the second my foot stepped inside the foyer. I slipped it from my pocket. "Joe, it's a text from Lauren."

"I'll let the dogs outside."

Lauren: Got e-mail about the mtng 2morrow night. Wish I cld be there. I'll watch on the computer.

Me: Oh, good! How are things?

Lauren: Funeral is this week.

Me: Remember Plan 7-C. We'll help any way we can.

Lauren: Rolling eyes emojis.

Me: I'm serious. How can I help?

Lauren: Mick inherited all the property. Please continue prayers.

Me: Lauren, that's terrific.

Lauren: Not sure it is. Fill you in later, Sis. Mick and I are driving to Cheyenne for overnight stay. Need a little time away from family. Crazy face emoji.

Me: Crazy face and heart emoji

* * *

I toddled out back where Joe tossed a ball to our hounds. "Lauren's watching the meeting online tomorrow night. It'll be 5:00 for her and Mick since they're on mountain time. She said Mick's inherited the ranch and asked for prayer."

"I just got the same request from Mick. Funny thing is, he's usually pretty sure of himself when it comes to real estate."

"Guess it's different when it's about his grandma's property."

"Bet you're right." He went inside, unclipped four leashes from their hooks in the mudroom, then returned outside. "Think I'll give those four long-legged canines a walk. Wanna come?"

I patted my tummy. "Come on, kiddos, we're off and running." I paused. "Well, maybe not running." I snickered.

The dogs saw the leashes and their tails whipped back and forth. My hubby gave the hand motion for them to sit, and they did. He clipped their leashes on their collars, and the four of them and two of us went out the back gate to explore. No sooner had we walked around the side of the Inn nearest the cottages, than the door to Q's and Sendy's cottage opened.

Uncle Quinn stood on the porch and shouted, "I told you I wasn't leaving Hope until Earnest finished the splash pad, but Sendy and I are checking out Tuesday morning and flying to Texas. Lucia's adopting a little boy in a couple days, and we want to be there."

Sendy joined him on the cottage porch. "We'll be back in a week or two and will need another reservation here. That's if y'all have a bungalow available."

I drifted toward the two of them. "We're so happy for y'all. Another grandchild is such a blessing. We'll hold a cottage for as long as you need." I stepped on the porch and hugged my uncle and Sendy. "Congrats to you both."

Sendy laughed. "Who would've thought we'd have another grandchild at our ages?"

Uncle Q guffawed. "We're still youngins', Sweetheart." He planted a smooch smack dab on Sendy's lips.

Joe reined in the dogs and stood beside me. "Y'all will be at the meeting tomorrow night. Right?"

"Nephew, we'll be there. As a matter of fact, after you walk those beasts, can we talk?"

Sendy teasingly punched his arm. "We've occupied these kids' time enough Papa Quirky." She held his hand. "Besides, Sea invited us for supper this evening. Remember?"

"Yep." He rubbed his jaw. "Let's talk tomorrow before the town hall meeting. Val let me know she has some horses we can use for riding classes. I wanna check them out before I go to Texas. I might need to transport a couple of horses from my ranch." He cocked his head. "Come ta think of it, Mick might have a few at his grandma's ranch in Wyoming, but it'd be easier to get local horses. For sure."

I stared at him. *Even I could've figured that out.*

Joe held tightly to our dogs' leashes. "I'll be at work till six tomorrow. Do you need me to go to Val's with you? I wouldn't be much help since I don't know anything about horses."

Uncle Q cringed. "Maybe it's about time you learned." He gave a slight wave. "See you tomorrow."

Sendy clung to Q's arm and whispered in his ear. He stopped mid stride and turned in our direction. "Joe, no need to worry about the horses. You're taking care of other stuff. See you tomorrow night at the meeting."

Ah, Sendy has corralled that buckin' bronco!

> *They also brought to the proper place their*
> *quotas of barley and straw for the chariot*
> *horses and the other horses. 1 Kings 4:28*

Chapter 24

Joe and I chatted as our canines trotted in front of us. Their eyes glued to the ducks in the pond and the squirrels scampering up a nearby magnolia tree. They didn't notice an orange feline sunbathing on the library porch railing.

"Joe, I wonder if that's one of the kittens we saw in the barn on Lauren's wedding day?"

He shrugged. "I'm glad we have more mousers around. Midnight was a pain at times, but she sure caught a lot of rodents."

"Ick. I don't even want to think of mice." We padded around the lake and stopped in front of his parent's home.

"Rae, I need to tell you something."

"What?"

"Dad said we can move into this house."

"Why?"

"Cause it's officially for the head of the university." The pups began to whine and yanked at their leashes. "We'd better get going."

"Joe, stop. I'm not leaving this spot till you answer this. Will your folks still have to move out of the house if we don't move in?"

"I'm not sure."

"Why are we just finding this out?"

"Dad called me and said he got an e-mail from the main campus the day before his retirement. It notified him about the possible move. He'd forgotten all about it and will tell Mom when they get back from their trip." Joe muttered. "Dad knew she'd worry about it."

"He's right." *I'm worried.*

* * *

My hubby and I finally arrived home and fed and watered the dogs. "Rae, we're trying to figure this out on our own. Prayer is the answer."

"How can you be so calm?"

He took me in his arms. "Because the Lord has everything lined up." He gently cupped my face in his hands. "Let's look at this as another adventure."

I grumbled. "I think we already have enough adventures. The Inn, your new job, babies on the way. I don't want anymore."

"Really? I don't believe you." He winked. "Let's throw caution to the wind." He pointed to the freezer. "Look in there."

I rolled my eyes and opened the drawer. "Joseph William Byer. You didn't."

"I did." He snatched two clean spoons from the dishwasher. "Your silverware, dear."

I snuggled close to him. "Buffalo Chips! I can't believe Uncle Q's ice cream flavor is my pregnancy craving. Thank you, Handsome! No offense or anything, but I don't want to share."

"Me either." He pulled a pint of chunky chocolate from the freezer. "I bought one of my favorites, too." He tapped my nose with the edge of his spoon. "And I'm not sharing either."

We sat on the porch swing. Sharing bites of our favorites with each other. Sugary sweet.

...Do not be afraid; do not be discouraged, for
the Lord your God will be with you wherever
you go Joshua 1:9.

Chapter 25

"Morning, Joseph." I kissed his cheek. "This is the day that the Lord has made…"

"Morning, Beautiful." He kissed my lips. "Let us rejoice and be glad in it."

"Are you a little scared?"

"Nope. Just concerned that I can't fill my dad's shoes." He scanned the living room. "Where are the dogs?"

"Outside. I fed and watered them while you were in the shower. Before you put on your dress shirt, lets have breakfast. It's ready on the table in the living room."

We sauntered to the table, bowed our heads in prayer, then tasted each morsel.

"Rae, this is delicious."

"Molly made the eggs and bacon." I poured him a cup of coffee. "But I did pop the bread into the toaster." I sniggled. "And added your favorite grape jelly."

"You like grape, too." He leaned over the table toward me. "Let me give you a grape smoocharoo."

Of course, I willingly obliged.

We crunched our bacon, savored every bite of scrambled eggs and toast, then finished our breakfast. Joe proceeded to wind his burgundy tie into a double Windsor knot, then added a suit coat to his muscular frame.

It was official. My hubby's first day in his new position. I waved to him from the front porch of the Inn. *I remember standing on the porch at my Pecan Street rental when I first moved to Hope, and you walked by. I gave you a cup of java and was mortified to speak with you. Now I'm mesmerized.*

* * *

My phone buzzed. "Hey, Lauren, are you and Mick doing all right?"

"We are but I'm calling to find out how you and Joe are this morning? His first day in his new job must be a little daunting and exciting. A new adventure."

"I don't know about all this adventure stuff, Sis. I told Joe I don't want anymore. We have the Inn, his job, and babies coming..." Silence.

"What else? I know you well enough to suspect there's more to this story. Spill the beans, Rae."

"Joe said there's a possibility we'll move into his folk's house since that's where the head of the university lives. Nothing's set in concrete. We'll find out more when his parents' get home."

"I see what you mean. The Inn is your home. I don't blame you for being concerned. As simple as it sounds, Mick and I will pray specifically about that."

"Thanks. Here I am whining and whimpering. Talk to me."

"The property here is beautiful. Wide open spaces with more stars in the sky than I've ever seen." She giggled. "Mick tells me we see the same stars in Hope, we just have nothing blocking them here. On a side note, we had a Milk Can dinner last night! It's like a Low Country boil but with different meats and veggies. It was delicious and I didn't have to help!" She paused.

"That sounds wonderful, and the Milk Can dinner sounds interesting." I laughed. "Milk Can and Low Country, who would've ever thought!" I snatched a tissue from my pocket and wiped my nose. "Maybe someday Joe and I'll get out that way." I hesitated. "Wait a minute. You're not planning on living there are you?"

"That's what I wanted to tell you. Mick will be here for the rest of the summer, and so will I. We'll make trips back and forth to Hope to make sure the builders are getting our home done."

"Joe and I can help with that. No worries about your home here."

"Thanks, Sis. There's a stipulation in the will. Grandma Alana specified she wants the bed and breakfast open again." She inhaled.

"What? Will y'all have to run it?" I trembled.

"We want to hire someone. But until then, who knows? First of all, it needs freshening up."

"Is it a dude ranch? Remember, Sis, I am an interior designer and love the details!"

"It's definitely not a dude ranch. Grandma Alana had an affinity for flower patterns and brocade. I'm desperate for ideas. I know your life is so busy, and I hesitate to ask about the decorating."

"Lauren, I'm never too busy to help. We're sisters and that's what sisters do. Right?"

"You're right, Sis." She sighed. "The B&B is beautiful but very outdated. I'll send pictures."

"I'd love to see them."

"Mick and I need all the help we can get. My mother-in-law is willing to assist, too, but she has told me over and over that she isn't a decorator. So, Rae, you're our go-to gal."

"I can't wait. And I'm not being sarcastic! My mind is already racing with ideas."

"Mick hired repairmen, painters, and a landscaping crew to renovate the outside of the property. They're locals and have worked together for years. They told me everything should be completed before the first snow in September."

"September?"

"Yep. It's crazy. Also, we need to hire somebody to manage the property." She cleared her throat. "Otherwise, Mick will stay here till we get someone. Guess you and I are having adventures we'd like to avoid."

"We are. Wonder what sage words Natalie would say to us right now?" I chortled.

"I miss Natalie. I even miss those crazy Historical Society ladies. No offense, I know you're one of them."

"You'll be part of the society when you get back from Wyoming. Don't think you can escape the clutches of the prestigious group."

"Did I tell you Emily sent me a text?"

"No. What did she say?"

"She's praying for Mick and me."

"That's precious."

"Then she added she'd take up the slack and look after you while I'm gone."

I gulped. "Lauren, that was so sweet of her."

"It was until she called me and offered to check on our home. She had a suggestion for the color palette."

"Shall I guess what color?"

We both blurted, "Pink!"

"Your sister-in-law is quite the character. I'm glad she's got your back, Rae." Lauren attempted to discreetly blow her nose. "Thanks for hearing me out. Mick and I'll be on the computer tonight for the meeting. Wish we could be there in person. I love the idea of lawn chairs, and hors d'oeuvres."

"Love you, Lauren. We're in this together."

"We sure are. Love you, too."

...But as for me, I trust in you. Psalms 55:23

Chapter 26

Lawn chairs dotted the grounds near the buildings. Uncle Quinn placed a makeshift lectern under a pecan tree, and Sendy situated a computer on top. Kramer and Nathaniel parked their golf cart utility truck under a weeping willow and unloaded ice chests filled with bottled water. Dr. Duntworth and Abel Dells discussed business on the porch of one of the buildings. Hopeites perused each of the buildings while nibbling on tapas.

The ladies in the society quick stepped in my direction. Opal patted my shoulder. "Everything will go well, Dear. We've already toured the structures and have a gazillion ideas."

"Don't scare our newest member in the society, Opal." Lottie tapped her finger to her chin. "Although Grace sent us a few ideas she has up her sleeve."

Anne added, "And they're the same things we thought about. We don't want you to stress over any of this, Rae. We're all excited about possibilities."

I did a double take when Emily scampered to my side. "Emily! Your hair is adorable. When did you get it cut?"

"This morning. I haven't shown mother yet." She cringed.

Natalie scootched around the other ladies and stood beside the two of us. "Does Blake like it?"

Em adjusted the glittery barrette in her hair. "He does."

"Then, that's all that matters." She wound her salt and pepper locks into a messy bun, then looked at me. "How can I help?"

"Pray, please."

Natalie winked, "Oh, Mrs. Byer, no worries in that area. God's got it covered."

Molly joined the swarm of women. "Kelly can't be here but will watch on her phone." She wiped a bead of perspiration from her forehead. "Wasn't it the sweetest thing that Kramer delivered water? He's such a great example for his little brother, Nathaniel. Sweet Rae, how can I help?"

I didn't get a chance to respond because Mayor Sounds lifted a bullhorn to his lips and bellowed into the contraption. "Ladies and gentlemen of Hope, South Carolina. Welcome to this town hall meeting. Without further ado, I'll turn this over to Joe, Rae, Quinn, and Sendy." He started to lay down the megaphone then pushed it close to his mouth. "Those of you on the computer, can you hear me?"

We could hear Grace and Lance respond. "Yes, and you're too loud."

Then Lauren and Mick added, "Yes, and we agree with the Byers."

Uncle Quinn stood under the pecan tree. "I don't need any bullhorn," he blurted.

The crowd applauded. Blake's dad, Gentry, added, "Isn't that the truth?" Everyone laughed.

Pastor David prayed. The meeting commenced.

* * *

Yvette Duntworth stood. "Hey, y'all." She paused. "I have an idea for that first building."

Dr. Duntworth added, "Speak up, Vetti. No need to be shy. Just tell 'em, dear."

Yvette, aka Vetti, glowered at her hubby, "Doodles, I'm not being shy, I'm just measuring my words."

The crowd roared with laughter and Quinn thundered, "Doodles!"

Yvette snatched the megaphone to her lips, "My suggestion for the first building is for Art classes. As y'all know, Anne is an artist and I'm an instructor." She motioned for Anne to stand under the tree with her and she darted to Yvette's side. "The two of us could actually run the classes, but we don't want to step on anyone's toes."

Joe stood next to the two women. "Is there anyone else with an idea for the first building? FYI: that building is equipped with an industrial sink."

The residents chitter-chattered for a bit then Victoria rang a bell she'd brought with her. "Joe, Rae, Quinn, and Sendy, we have a consensus. We've decided, but of course y'all have the final say." She fanned herself with a vintage funeral home fan. "We love the idea of that building being used for art." She turned toward the crowd. "Right, y'all?"

"Hear, hear!"

Joe, Quinn, Sendy, and I talked quickly among ourselves. We all gave a thumbs up, then Joe added, "It's done. The building is an art building. Anne and Yvette, we'll text y'all about a meeting next week at the Inn. When you do come, please bring detailed plans."

The two ladies practically floated back to their chairs. Martha Ingles, the State Historic Preservation Office official, stood. "Ladies and gentlemen, I'm thrilled to say none of those buildings are historical. Things should be underway quickly."

Everyone applauded.

Martha continued, "Several of us with children came up with an idea for the second building. It's noticeably larger than the first." She sipped from her water bottle. "Dance classes."

A few guttural moans filtered through the air.

Quinn put up his hand. "Let Martha speak."

"I know dance isn't a priority for many, but music classes for children could be included in that building, too." She motioned for Molly and Fran to come forward. "We put our heads together and came up with a design." She grinned. "Go ahead, Molly."

Molly smiled. "As many of you know, my Kelly loves to sing. Even though she can't be at this meeting in person she's watching on her phone." She walked closer to the lectern and spoke to the computer. "Right, sweetheart?"

We heard Kelly's voice, "Yes, Mother." She cleared her throat. "Everyone, I'm not being presumptuous to think I can teach music to children, but I'd love the opportunity. I want to give back to the community. Y'all have encouraged me since I was an itsy-bitsy girl, and I'd like to do the same for your children and grandchildren. That is, if you go along with my mom and the other ladies' ideas."

Fran interjected, "Kelly is so talented, and my children love her to pieces."

Sea spoke from the back row of lawn chairs. "I love that idea, but who's going to teach dance?"

Hannah, Natalie's daughter, raised her hand. "Many of you know I've taken lessons since I was three. I'm obviously not a professional since I work at Peaches and Cream and serve ice cream."

Everyone cheered!

Shelly Rodriguez stood next to Hannah. "Y'all know Javier and I run Fenster Haus but might not know I am a ballerina. I've danced all my life and when my husband and I married, had babies, then bought Fenster Haus, I gave up that career to pursue another. I'd love the opportunity to teach dance part-time alongside Hannah."

I grabbed the megaphone off the lectern. "I am absolutely amazed at all the talent in this tiny town. Maybe we can have recitals in the rec center when we ever get started on that huge building. Oops, guess I'm getting ahead of myself." I twaddled.

Quinn patted me on the shoulder. "Niece, we haven't even voted yet."

Sendy patted him on the shoulder. "Husband, she's fully aware of that. I love Rae's enthusiasm."

Joe kissed my cheek and motioned for the bullhorn. "Please take time to talk amongst yourselves about the music and dance suggestions."

Mr. Ike raised his hand. "You know what? We don't need any more discussion, do we friends?"

"Hear, hear!"

Ike smiled that toothy grin of his. "My granddaughter, Penny, asked me the other day if she could learn to sing like Miss Kelly and dance like a ballerina she saw on TV. I can honestly say, you'd make Penelope happy, so that would make me feel the same."

I sauntered to where he sat and hugged his fragile shoulders. "Mr. Ike, you're such a wonderful Papa."

Joe, Sendy, and Quinn spoke in unison. "Second building, Music and Dance."

The crowd applauded.

Texas Quinn swiveled his eyes toward Joe and folded his muscled arms across his chest. "Nephew and everybody else, hear me out." He pulled Sendy close to his side and kissed the top of her head. "This little lady and I have an idea for the third building. It's nothing fun."

Dr. Duntworth bellowed. "TQ, whatever you come up with me and my team can do it." He pulled his infamous rag from his overall pocket and wiped his forehead.

"We need a building for storage."

Sendy clung to Q's arm as she stepped on top of a tree stump. "I hope y'all can see and hear me. It doesn't sound glamorous, but we need the storage space."

Joe drew a little closer to his uncle and Sendy, then pointed at the crowd. "What do y'all think?"

Several in the crowd mumbled for a few minutes, then Natalie grabbed the bullhorn and stood on tip toe. "We have a consensus. We're with y'all. It's a good suggestion. That way the other buildings will have all the space for classes."

Abel Dells interjected. "The smallest building on the property should be bathrooms."

A loud "ugh" came from a few folks until Abel Dells spoke into the bullhorn and explained the reason. After a little convincing, there was a unanimous decision. The vote passed.

Mayor Sounds shoved out of his folding chair and traipsed to where we stood. "Ladies and gentlemen. Let's take a break. When we return, we'll discuss the name of our newfound land. We'll return in fifteen minutes."

* * *

When everyone returned to their chairs, lightening streaked across the sky and thunder boomed overhead.

Mayor Sounds bellowed, "Meeting adjourned!"

Uncle Quinn grabbed the computer. Joe and Blake shoved the boards used for the lectern into the back of Blake's truck and threw a tarp over them. Emily climbed inside the vehicle and waved as she and her hubby drove away. All the residents ran to their cars within seconds of the downpour. Uncle Q and Sendy yelled for us to get in their vehicle. We were glad we did.

Quinn laughed. "Y'all would've been drowned rats if you hadn't got in this truck."

That's not a great visual, Uncle Quinn.

* * *

We trudged inside and comforted our canines. Buddy and Puffs rested quietly on the foyer rug, but Trixie and Heidi nervously traipsed back and forth. Joe fluffed their ears while I filled their bowls with water.

"Joe, want anything to drink?" I looked out the kitchen window. "Professor, come see what Uncle Q and Sendy are doing."

"Not sure I want to." He rolled his eyes and glared out the window. "Guess they're not concerned about the severe thunderstorm and tornado watch." Q and Sendy snuggled on the cottage porch swing.

* * *

Joe and I popped popcorn, grabbed a couple orange juices, and headed up the back stairs toward our domain.

I scrunched into the sofa cushion, put my tootsies on the coffee table and nibbled my buttery popcorn. "Professor, we never got ideas for the name of the land. We don't need another meeting. Do we?"

He took a swig of his juice. "Folks can text suggestions to us. Agree?"

"Yes, but let's do something fun. Maybe a box on the Inn porch where people can drop their name ideas in?" I planted my feet on the floor and pushed off the sofa.

"Okay with me. But who'll make the box?"

"That's easy. I'll see if some of the kiddos in town can help. Sorting the names and picking one will be tricky. Don't want any hurt feelings."

Joe pulled his phone from his pocket. "I'll send a text to Q now. See if it's a go."

Joe got a response within seconds.

Quinn: Agree. No texting tonight. Turning off our phones. I suggest you do the same. Night.

We didn't need any advice from our uncle. Popcorn, soft music, and time for the two of us was just what we wanted. Our fur babies sat attentively nearby just waiting for a popcorn morsel or two. *Togetherness.*

Gather the people, consecrate the assembly…
Joel 2:16

Chapter 27

I sent a text to parents who had little ones to see if their children would like to help with the box. Then I sent an e-mail explaining the entire idea about picking a name for the recreation area to all the Hope-ites.

Within a short while, Val responded reluctantly that her boys weren't really interested in the box. Mr. Wood informed me Penelope cartwheeled through the house with excitement. Fran let me know her daughters were ecstatic, but her son wasn't. She offered to use her front porch as the decorating station since she had a large box, a ton of markers, paste, stickers, and wrapping paper. All I needed to do was inform everyone when the box was on the porch and ready for name ideas.

* * *

I'd had Collette Timble on my mind and sent her a text:
Me: Would you like to join me for lunch today?
Within seconds I received her response.
Collette: That'd be great!
Me: Is 11:30 okay?
Collette: Absolutely. Baby-friendly place?
Me: Burger King?
Collette: Sounds wonderful. I can drive since I have the car seat.
Me: I didn't think of that. We can go locally and meet somewhere.

Collette: I'll drive. Heading to Greenville sounds fantastic!

I need to get myself mentally prepared for babies. Two car seats in a VW Bug?

* * *

I waddled down the porch steps and entered Collette's van. "It's so good to see you both." I peeked over the seat at beautiful Daisy. "Oh, my goodness, she has a bottom tooth!"

"She sure does. Teeth and nursing can be a little challenging at times." She cringed. "You'll find that out soon enough!" She put the van in drive and off we sped toward lunchtime in Greenville.

"Rae, how are you feeling? You look fabulous, by the way."

"I'm feeling great now that morning sickness is behind me."

"I understand completely." She fanned herself with a tissue. "Baby hormones are taking over!"

"What did you say?"

"Yep, you heard me right. I'm due in late February. These babies will be a year apart. Not the way we planned, but Earnie keeps reminding me God has it covered."

"That's so exciting!" I twisted around in the seat and looked at Daisy in her car seat. "If your second is anything like that baby doll... Come to think of it, I'll be thrilled if even one of mine is as sweet as your Daisy."

Collette parked in front of the Burger King entrance, and I watched as she maneuvered everything needed to appease baby Daisy while we ate. It amazed me how she didn't even flinch as she balanced diaper bag and baby carrier with precision and grace.

We ordered our meals at the counter then slid into a booth. Our hamburger and fries might not have been the healthiest of meals, but we loved building a long-lasting relationship and friendship.

"Collette, you amaze me."

"What do you mean?" She popped a ketchupy fry into her mouth.

"You take care of Daisy with such ease and you're pregnant!"

"Rae, you amaze me. You're expecting twins!"

"I guess we're both pretty amazing, if pregnancy is the prerequisite!" I joked as I took the last bite of my burger. "By the way, want a shake? My grandma and I always used to treat ourselves with one any chance we'd get."

"Of course. Calcium!"

"My treat."

Daisy slept soundly during the meal and on the drive home. Friendship—such a wonderful thing.

* * *

My phone buzzed as I walked inside the Inn. I fished inside my purse for my cell then snatched it out just before it went to voicemail.

Call from Dr. Duntworth. "I called Joe but no answer. Plans for the dorm building need to be revised. Martha Ingles came by to say--."

"Oh no, it's historical, isn't it?" I winced.

"No." He cleared his throat. Loudly. "We're good. Wanted you and Joe to know Abel and I used that old building as a test case this morning."

"That's great news about the dorms." I sighed. "What kind of case?"

"A test case. Our summer students at the university examined the entire structure for their exam earlier today. And they got points for any structural concerns they found."

"Really? What did they find?"

"They passed but the dorm didn't. No surprise to me and Abel. Whole thing needs to be demolished."

"Dr. D, I'll slip on my boots and be there in a few."

"I'm not at the land. I'm at the university and heading home. Give the message to Joe, please." His voice muffled. "No need, Joe just stepped into my office." Call ended.

Within minutes I received a call from Lauren. "Rae, guess you heard about the dorm."

"Dr. Duntworth just told me. I can't believe you heard it all the way out in Wyoming!"

"He sent me a text early this morning. Remember I'm on Mountain Time?" She yawned. "He asked me..." Lauren yawned a second time, "If my students want to help with the building project. I reminded him I'm not teaching summer courses."

"Now, I'm yawning, too."

"Guess what else he said?"

"What?"

Lauren cleared her throat. "These are his exact words. 'If you can come back to Hope before the fall semester, we need your expertise.'"

"I agree with him."

"Guess what again."

"I'm out of guesses."

"After I spoke to Dr. Duntworth, Mick came into the kitchen and told me about a realtor convention he wants to go to. He could have done it on the computer, but he feels in-person would be much better." She took a deep breath.

"Where is it going to be?"

"In Greenville! I told Mick about the possibility of being on the team with Dr. D and Abel, and he's ecstatic for me. So, I wanted to get y'all's opinion before setting anything in concrete."

"Are you kidding me? Now I'm ecstatic!" My phone buzzed. "Oh, Sis, Joe's calling me. Mind if I call you back?"

"Not at all. We'll talk later. Love ya!"

Joe relayed exactly what Dr. D and Lauren had said to me. "What do ya think, Beautiful?"

"I think we should include Lauren. It's not just because she'll spend more time in Hope and I love her dearly. I know she's more than qualified."

"I'll send a text to Uncle Q and get his feedback. Love you, Gorgeous. Bye."

I placed my phone on the counter, washed an apple, and crunched it in nervous anticipation. Then my phone chimed the familiar tune indicating the professor was on the line.

"Joseph, what did he say?"

"It's a go."

"I'll let Lauren know! Love you, Hunk!"

"Love you, too, Mrs. Byer."

In their hearts humans plan their course, but the Lord establishes their steps. Proverbs 16:9

Chapter 28

My phone buzzed at 6:30 a.m. I sat on the side of the bed and took it off the nightstand. I noticed a text from my mother-in-law to all the Historical Society ladies.

Grace: Wake up ladies. On-line meeting today at 11 concerning July 4

Me: Everything okay?

Grace: Thumbs up. Plan 2D is in effect.

Me: I'll be on-line at 11. Thx

Mine was the only response. *The rest of the ladies must be asleep. Wish I was.* I didn't dare ask what Plan 2D was. I'd skim through my trusty Historical Society handbook.

Joe yawned, stretched, then pulled himself out of bed. "Everything all right?" The dogs jumped from the bed to the wooden floor and trotted toward the doggy door in our upstairs domain.

"Your mom sent all the society ladies a text at 6:30. I thought something was wrong until she wrote she's hosting an on-line meeting at eleven today. Something to do with the fourth of July."

Joe stretched his muscled arms above his head. "She needs to give up some control. Sorry about the early wakeup. I'll let the dogs out. Then do you wanna walk to Bitty's Buns for breakfast?"

"That's a fabulous idea."

The dogs and Joe trotted downstairs while I got ready for breakfast at the bakery.

* * *

I dressed in mint green shorts and a melon-colored t-shirt. Joe helped tie my tennis shoes.

We held hands, sauntered down the driveway, and turned onto Beaufort Street. "Joe, look over there." I pointed. "Penelope is doing a great job walking Rosebud, but Mr. Ike can't keep up."

"Looks like Rosebud inherited Puffs' and Buddy's affinity for the lake and ducks. I'll run and help." He sprinted in their direction.

I noticed Penny's gargantuan Labradane pup pulling her toward the water. Then I glanced at Mr. Wood as he leaned on his walker. *Lord, I'm concerned about Mr. Ike.*

Joe saved the day and guided Rosebud toward Bitty's Buns as Penny skipped ahead of him. Mr. Ike Wood and I sauntered to a metal table and chairs outside the bakery.

Natalie opened the shop door and scooted outside. "You came along just in time, Joe. Rosebud might have jumped in that lake like Buddy and Puffs did last year." She giggled. "Now what can I get y'all?" She patted Penny on the top of her head. "I made some fresh blueberry muffins, sweet girl. I know they're your favorite. Would you like one?"

Penny looked at her Papa. "Is that okay, Papa?" She hugged his neck and gave him a peck on the cheek.

Mr. Wood leaned back in his chair. "Thanks for asking, Granddaughter. You'll be going to first grade soon Pens, so you can make the decision." He patted her hand.

"Miss Natalie, I'd love a blueberry muffin and chocolate milk, please." She reached for her puppy. "And Rosebud would like fresh water, please."

Natalie winked at Mr. Ike. "She's growing up, Papa, isn't she?"

Ike smiled. "She sure is and I'm proud of her."

Natalie petted Rosebud then offered her hand to Penny. "Why don't you come inside with me young lady and help me get breakfast?" She glanced at the rest of us. "Do y'all want your usuals?"

The three of us nodded in unison. Then the soon-to-be first grader grinned from ear to ear and walked inside with Natalie.

Within seconds Ike Wood cleared his throat. "You both must notice I'm not in the best of shape. Crazy hip. I'm trying my hardest to keep up with Penny, but it's getting more and more difficult. Guess that's obvious."

I scooted my chair closer to him. "How can we help? We'll do whatever you need."

Joe added, "Rae is right. We'll do what you need, Mr. Ike."

"It will be easier when Mick's parents return from Wyoming. His mom comes over each morning and gets my granddaughter's breakfast. She comes back in the evening and gets Penny ready for bed."

I placed a hand on my tummy. "I never knew that."

He chuckled. "Not many people do." He shifted in his chair.

* * *

Penny and Natalie delivered our meals. Fortunately, the cooler morning air kept the smoldering summer heat at bay. Natalie raised a black-and-white striped umbrella over our table, placed a thermos of coffee, and carafe of orange juice on the hot pink linen tablecloth.

She poured cold water into a plastic bowl and set it in front of Rosebud.

The Bitty's Buns owner winked. "Bon Appetit, y'all. Just text me if you need anything and I'll be here." She patted Ike on the knee. "Mr. Ike, your Penny's quite the helper, kind and good. She plated the meals and even reminded me to bring napkins."

Ike smiled and cleared his throat. "Penelope, I spoke to Miss Natalie the other day on the phone. We were wondering if you would like to visit the bakery every once in a while, to help decorate cookies and cupcakes."

He removed his baseball cap and placed it on his lap.

The enormous butterfly shaped bow on Penelope's head bobbed up and down. "Yes! Yes, Papa!" She jumped from her chair and almost tripped over Rosebud's leash. "I'm giving you an extra big hug." She placed her tiny hands around her Papa's neck. "I want to help."

Natalie smiled and patted her hand to her heart. "Such great news. Now I'm heading inside, y'all. Just text if you need anything." She meandered slowly up the steps, and into Bitty's Buns.

Joe put his fork on his plate. "You're a great example, Mr. Ike."

He cocked his head. "Me? Why?"

"You have a good heart and are a great man."

Penny sniggled. "Papa is the best Papa ever isn't he, Mr. Joe?"

"Yes, he is."

A good man brings good things out of the good
stored up in his heart... Luke 6:45

Chapter 29

Grace tapped her water goblet with a spoon to bring the video meeting to order. "Y'all look so funny in all those squares. Well, I guess they're really in the shape of rectangles."

Victoria snickered. "President, Grace. You're in a rectangle too. Shall we proceed?"

Grace grimaced. "Ladies, I'm concerned about July 4th. Lance tried to reassure me everything will fall into place without us being in Hope. I'm worried."

Lottie interjected. "Dear, we follow Plan 2D every year. No worries. We'll miss you and Lance, but we'll keep you informed. We won't hesitate to call on you if we have any questions." She adjusted her glasses on the tip of her nose. "Right, y'all!"

"Right!"

These ladies spoke with such finesse and experience. They reassured my mom-in-law there was absolutely nothing to be anxious about.

Until Emily mumbled something under her breath, "Fireworks cancelled." Then gasped and put her hand across her mouth.

Grace tripped over her tongue. "W-what did you say, Baby Girl?"

"Nothing, Mother."

"No fireworks. I know I heard you right. After all, I did birth you and I know your mumbles." She pursed her lips. "We can't celebrate without the fireworks display over the lake. It just won't be tradition, ladies."

I bit my lip.

Anne blurted, "We will come up with a plan. It will still be Independence Day with or without fireworks. You know what, Grace, this is your time and Lance's, so please don't fret. Enjoy your trip. Everything will be okay because we Historical Society Ladies will improvise as we've done in the past."

Emily added. "God's got this, Mother. By the way, I love the pictures you sent. Colorado is beautiful." She patted her nose with a tissue. "Have fun. I love you and Daddy."

Grace rapped the goblet again with her spoon. "I love you too, Sweet Girl. Ladies, you must keep me informed. You're the best and I miss y'all tons. But I must admit, I'm thoroughly enjoying this time with Lance." She winked. "Meeting adjourned!"

* * *

Emily called me. "Rae, let's go to Peaches and Cream for lunch."

"Ice cream for lunch?"

"We're expecting and we need calcium. Wanna meet there in about fifteen minutes?"

"See you in a few." I slipped into my flip flops, headed out the back door, and noticed Joe in the yard. "Joseph, you're as dirty as the hounds!"

"I'm giving them a bath." He aimed the hose at me in jest. "Come help me." His eyebrows bobbed up and down.

"Don't even try it, Mr." I patted my baby bump. "You wouldn't want to get our children wet." I carefully manuevered down the steps and out the back gate to avoid the wet dogs. "I can't, Prof. I'm joining your sister for lunch."

"Bring me back a sandwich or something, please."

"Want ice cream? We're going to Peaches and Cream."

"That's not a lunch place."

"I told your sister almost the same thing, but she assured me we pregnant women need calcium."

"She's crazy!" He started to rinse the mongrels. "Have fun, Honey."

"If you don't spray me, I'll give you a kisseroo!" I gave him two kisses.

* * *

The bell above the door at Peaches and Cream jingled as I stepped inside. My sis-in-law chatted at the counter with Hannah and Sidney, then turned in my direction. "Hey, Rae, my treat today. Order whatever you want." She licked a wooden sample spoon filled with pink ice cream.

"Thanks, Em. I'm going for something different today."

Sidney stood with eyes goggled. "You never order anything different. Now I know you're expecting a baby!"

I patted my bulging middle. "As if you haven't noticed?"

Hannah piped up. "In that case, Mrs. Rae, maybe you'd like to try one of our summer flavors. Beachball Melon might be your flavor of choice!" Her face turned beet red.

We all laughed hysterically while some of the other customers joined in the fun.

Emily purchased a waffle cone filled with three scoops of Cotton Candy Pink Cherry. I nixed the Beachball Melon idea but did opt for two scoops of Belly Flop Banana in a sugar cone. Of course, we all chuckled at the new flavor I'd chosen.

Emily and I plopped onto ice cream parlor chairs, then the bell above the door jingled. Sea entered the shop and waved to us.

She sauntered the short distance to where we sat. "Look at you two baby bump girls. See y'all are getting your calcium." She twittered.

Emily and I laughed then I patted the chair next to me. "Please join us, Sea. We hardly ever get time to visit."

"Sure, wish I could, but I need to get home to pack for my trip."

Em swallowed another bite of her pink ice cream. "I didn't know you were going anywhere because my mother is out of town. She would have informed me." She grinned.

I blurted, "She would have informed everyone."

Sea added, "That's for sure." She sashayed to the counter, placed her order, then stopped at our table. "You know what? I have a few minutes to chit chat." She slid into the chair next to me.

I nibbled another bite of my Belly Flop Banana delight. "So where are you going, Sea?"

She sat back in the metal chair. "Izzy and Grady invited me to their new home. I'm so excited. I'll be there two weeks and offered to watch my grandchildren so the two of them can have a second honeymoon."

Emily licked her cone then wiped her mouth with a napkin. "This must be second honeymoon time since my folks are on one, too." She took a crunchy bite of her waffle cone.

Sea added. "You're right, Emily. Guess who's watching Angels to Zithers while I'm gone?" She didn't wait for an answer. "Blake's mom, Tilly. My trip is so last minute, and she was just precious to agree to run things."

Emily spluttered. "My mother-in-law? I didn't know she ever went to your store."

Sea laughed. "Bless your heart, dear. She runs my website and knows every aspect of the shop. So, I can rest assured all will be well." She finished her cup of sherbet. "Well, girls, I'm off. See you in a couple of weeks."

Emily fumbled with her cone. "I wonder if Blakey knows his mom is helping at the store?"

I consumed the last bite of my calcium-filled lunch. "I hate to change the subject, but I am anyway. Do you know anything about Plan 2D? I haven't looked through our historical pamphlet."

"I don't know a thing about it either." She smirked. "Maybe we can come up with our own plan."

We both knew that was never happening. After all, the Historical Society had a plan for everything. Almost.

I sauntered back to the Inn and Emily headed toward home. I had a feeling she'd stop at Angels to Zithers to peek in on her mother-in-law.

*For there is a proper time and procedure for
every matter... Ecclesiastes 8:6*

Chapter 30

"Morning Has Broken" played in the Inn kitchen as Molly hummed along with the beautiful choral arrangement. She pivoted in my direction, "Oh, my goodness, Rae, you surprised me." She turned the music down.

"Louder please, Molly. That's one of my favorite hymns. I wish you'd sing out like your Kelly has done."

She picked up a cookie crumb dotted spatula and used it as a mic. I snatched a wooden spoon from a glass utensil holder and the two of us sang reverently until the next song on her playlist. *"Surfin' USA."* Molly and I roared with laughter as we attempted to keep up with the beat. When the song ended, we both gulped a glass of water till the next song started.

Joe snuck up behind me, wrapped his arms around my rotund waist, and swayed with me as I attempted to stay focused on the words *"Humble and Kind."* To no avail. My wooden spoon dropped onto the counter, and I turned in his direction and the two of us did our own rendition of slow dancing.

Molly sat on a stool. No spatula in her hand, just a tissue.

Joe halted in his tracks. "Miss Molly, are you okay?"

"I am. Just a little advice, though. Don't forget to take time to dance and love each other. Time slips away much too quickly."

The Lord's timing is always perfect. Our back door opened and in walked Molly's hubby, Henry. He paused then looked at her. "I've been looking for you, Sweetheart, and when you didn't answer your phone, I got concerned."

Molly slipped off the stool, Henry took her in his arms, and the two more seasoned romantics swayed to each word. Tears flowed down Molly's cheeks. I wasn't sure, but my thoughts strayed to her upcoming surgery. Maybe her tender tears were spurred not only by the past but by the future, too.

* * *

Fran arrived in her Buds and Blooms van. The back hatch lifted, and she slipped on her gardening gloves. "Hey, Rae. I did something different for the cottages. Hope you like it." She pulled one of two boxes out of the back. "Come see."

"You know I love everything you do." I peeked inside. "The flowerpots are gorgeous!"

"Guess who made them?" she continued. "Well, I'll tell you because you'll never guess. Anne and Yvette. They made them a couple years ago, and I'm embarrassed to say I put them in the storage shed behind my shop."

"They're perfect. Let me help you get the other box."

"No, dear, you're carrying two babies and that's enough."

I glowered at her. "You're pregnant, too. I thought we mamas had to stick together."

She beamed. "Guess I hadn't thought about that." The van doors slid open. "I've got my trusty collapsible wagon." She pulled it out of the van. "Rae, be honest with me."

"I always am." I smiled.

"Zoe and Olivia are at home and George needs to go back to work after lunch. Is it okay if the girls ride their bikes here and help me pot a few flowers? Before you answer, they want Penelope to come, too." She pulled the wagon to the first cottage and sat on the top step. "Guess I'm a little more winded than usual."

"First of all, Fran, you never have to ask me about having the kiddos help or anything else for that matter. I'd love to have all three girls come over. What's Clark doing? He's welcome, too."

"No way, as he'd say. Any time he gets freedom from his sisters and one-on-one time with his Labradane pup, Alfie, my boy is thrilled." She made a call to George and let him know all the girls could come to the Inn.

"Fran, I'm going inside to get cookies for the girls. Molly made them earlier and I want to try them too. See you in a few."

She gave me a thumbs-up and proceeded to set an empty flowerpot on each cottage porch.

* * *

I put two chocolate chunk cookies into individual baggies, snatched some floral paper napkins off the counter, filled a thermos with milk, and added paper cups to the bag. My fur babies whined and whimpered as I slid into my flip flops.

"Silly pups. Wanna come with me?" They wiggled and jiggled when I opened the back door, flew down the steps, and sat upon command. "You know what, you sweet things, no leashes today. Just follow me."

I opened the back gate and Buddy led the way as only the patriarch of the pack could do. The girls spotted the four long legged hounds then ran back and forth in the yard till the puppies tired and sprawled on the porch.

Fran motioned for her daughters and Penelope to sit on a cottage porch step. "Okay, y'all. You've had lots of exercise. Now let's get down to business and have more fun!" She giggled. "Please put on gardening gloves and I'll show you what we need to do."

The youngsters followed her directions then filled each pot with hot pink geraniums.

I sat on the porch near them. "Fran, these girls are the best helpers ever. Thank you for bringing them."

Fran winked in my direction then nodded at the three little ones. "What do you say girls?"

"Thank you!" They chirped in unison.

"You're Wel..." I didn't get to finish.

Within seconds we noticed pellets of dirt landing nearby. When Fran's son, Clark, ran through the front yard with Val, the vet's, four boys, we knew where the dirt came from.

Fran's oldest daughter, Zoe, picked up a handful of potting soil, drew her arm back in full pitching mode, and landed a glob of the gritty stuff at her brother's feet.

Fran glared at Zoe, then cupped her hands around her mouth and whistled. "You boys get over here!" She turned and winked at me. "Guess big brother, Clark, misses his sisters already."

All the boys ran to Fran and stopped in their tracks. I watched how she corralled five sweaty boys. "You fellas clean up the dirt. Ask Mrs. Rae if she has a broom you can use." She pivoted in Zoe's direction. "Please scoop up the potting soil and put it in that last pot over there."

All of them squirmed, then said in unison, "Yes, Ma'am."

I pointed the boys toward our backyard. "There are a couple brooms in the shed you can use. Mind taking the dogs with y'all and putting them in the yard?"

"Yes, Ma'am." Off they trotted with dogs following close behind.

"Fran, I need any parental advice you can offer."

She glanced their way then back at me. "You did great with them, Rae."

"I'm learning." I laughed. "Mind if I get cookies for the boys?"

"They'd love it."

I fast walked to the Inn, got the snack, and returned to the scene of the crime. The boys swept up the mess, washed their hands with the hose, and devoured their chocolate chunk cookies before they darted to Val's. The gals rode their bikes back to Fran's home to eat their sweet snacks.

Fran hugged my neck. "Thanks for putting up with all the chaos today. The girls and I'll start decorating the drop box for name ideas for the recreation area this afternoon.

"I thoroughly enjoyed myself! Thanks, Fran."

* * *

After Joe got off work, we walked to the land. He unlocked the door to our newly appointed Art studio. "I'm excited about the possibilities in here and the dance studio."

We kicked the dirt where the corral was almost completed. Joe pointed to the trenches for the splash pad water pipes. "Rae, Earnest says his goal is to finish the project before July 4th. He's recruited more workers to finish on time."

"That'll be super!"

We meandered toward the Inn, and I stopped under a pecan tree. "Joseph, I remember thinking when I saw these trees I'd make pecan pies and I haven't made one."

"Hmm, wife, this year you can make them since you'll have so much idle time at Thanksgiving." He squiggled his brows sarcastically.

"That's right. I'll either be pregnant or already have twins. Yes, plenty of time for baking." I jostled his arm in jest as we ambled home.

* * *

"Professor, we're having lemon chicken, rice, and broccoli for supper tonight. Mind setting the table?" I placed my phone in a basket on the counter.

"Paper plates?"

"Let's live dangerously and use real ones." I toddled into the dining room and removed my grandma's dinner plates from the French sideboard. "Let's use these. If my grandma were here, she'd say, 'Why save special items just for guests? Remember, family is special, too.'" I handed him two robin's egg blue vintage dinner plates. "Look at the tiny pink peonies outlining the border. These were her favorites. Now they're mine, too."

"Want me to put a tablecloth on that table?" He pointed to one of the small tables nestled in the corner near the windows.

"Dear Husband, you're quite the designer." I reached into the sideboard drawer, plucked out an antique Battenberg lace tablecloth and handed it to him.

We served ourselves buffet style since there wasn't much room for serving dishes at the romantic table for two. Joe removed two crystal goblets from the hutch and placed them with precision near our dishes.

He pulled out my chair, and I managed to cozy into the seat. "Beautiful, we need to do this more often. I like having you to myself occasionally." He winked. "Actually, I love having you alone all the time." He kissed the top of my head, then slid into his chair.

"You spoil me, Professor."

We bowed our heads to pray, and my handsome prince's phone buzzed. "Rae, I noticed your cell is in the kitchen, excuse me. I'm putting mine there, too. No interruptions tonight." He left the table and returned quickly without his cell. He prayed over our meal. *Thank You, Lord.*

Joe cut a piece of his chicken, added a hefty helping of broccoli to his fork, then managed to eat it in one huge bite. "Honey, this is great. Thank you for making a home-cooked meal." He palmed his forehead before I responded. "You've made me good meals before—"

"I knew what you meant." I started to take a bite of my chicken. "You know what? Maybe I should send a picture to your mother so she can see that I made you something from scratch."

He gulped a swig of water. "No way."

I chuckled. "Absolutely no way!"

I bit into my crunchy broccoli then proceeded to tell him about Fran and all the kiddos coming to the Inn to help. "She's such a fabulous mother and so patient. She managed Val's boys and her son when they started pelting dirt at the girls. She corrected Zoe, too, when she tried to retaliate."

"Sounds like Emily and me when we were kids." He finished the last bite of chicken. "You'll be a great mom. No worries." Crooked grin.

"And you'll be a fantastic dad." I wiped my mouth with my napkin. "I didn't make dessert, but there are still a few cookies left."

"No cookies for me. I'm stuffed. Sounds like it's been a good day." He shoveled his last bite of rice into his mouth.

"It has. Now tell me about yours."

"I had a couple meetings. I never realized until now all the things Dad did."

"What were your meetings about?"

"Just interviewing prospective professors. Stuff like that."

"You know what? I'm so proud of you." I took his hand in mine and gave a squeeze. "This time together has been more than good."

"How about I make your day even better? Why don't you go upstairs, and relax in the tub while I clean the dishes?"

"You're the best, Joe." I leaned in and kissed his cheek. "Thank you for taking care of me."

"Oh, you'd do well on your own, Wife, but I'm glad I get to be your trusty assistant."

I trudged upstairs, ran the water, and closed the bathroom door. I refused to be invaded by Puffs and Buddy, let alone Trixie and Heidi, too.

By the time Joe finished downstairs, I'd taken a relaxing bath, slipped into what my mother used to call, baby doll pajamas, and crawled into bed. I never sensed my handsome prince joining me for slumber. Sweet dreams.

So God created mankind in his own image, in the image of God he created them; male and female he created them. Genesis 1:27

Chapter 31

I woke up early and noticed Joe had already left for the university. There was a sticky note on the bathroom mirror.

Beautiful. Checked website before bed. Chandler's reserved cottage for tonight and tomorrow. Oh yeah, Kramer picked up the dogs and took them to Val's. BTW: I sorted through mail this a.m. Look in large envelope on the dresser.

I shuddered at the memory of Mrs. Chandler's snarky comments she made during her last visit, until I received a text from her daughter.

Martha: Sorry for late reservation

Me: No problem at all

Martha: Dad loves your place. Mom does, too. I'll try to be there when they arrive.

Me: No worries, friend. Smiley face emoji

The manila envelope was already opened. Inside were pictures of the dormitory and the smaller buildings when they were used by the university. I checked the return address on the mailer and noticed it was from Dr. and Mrs. Griddle. Tucked inside another envelope was a check and note. It read:

Joe, Rae, Quinn, and Sendy use this for whatever you need to complete your projects. Hope it helps. The Griddles.

I gasped and sent a text to Joe.

Me: I opened the envelope. I can't believe the Griddles' generous contribution!

Joe: Smiley face emoji

* * *

I nabbed a scone from the covered cake plate on the counter, poured a glass of milk, then flopped onto a stool at the island. I sent a text to Molly to let her know about guests for breakfast tomorrow. My mind raced at the thought of Mrs. Chandler's arrival. I finished my breakfast, moved at a clipped pace to cottage four where the Chandlers would stay, and straightened the butter yellow sheets to perfection. I opened the plantation shutters and refolded the extra towels in the linen closet, then made sure a traditional coffee pot sat squarely on the coffee bar. I slid the Keurig into the cabinet. Now Mrs. Chandler couldn't complain about the Keurig like she did last time. Water, juice, and soda filled the small fridge. After doing a thorough scan in every nook and cranny I felt assured Mrs. Chandler wouldn't complain.

My phone buzzed. Sendy.

"Rae, we'll be home..." She paused. "Quinn just reminded me home is in Texas, too. Crazy fella. Anyway, we'll be in Hope Friday night. Will you possibly have a cottage available?"

"Of course. There's always room."

"I have to tell you something."

"Are you pregnant?"

She bellowed, "I swanny, girl. Heavens no!"

"What is the something?" I twirled a strand of my hair almost into a knot.

"She whispered. "Can you keep a secret?"

"I-I'm not sure. Is it a good secret?"

"Rae Long Byer, I just found this out," she muttered. "Has Lauren called you?"

"Not today. Is she okay?"

"Absolutely. As you know, my son lives in Wyoming with his family. Mick is interviewing him about running his grandma's bed and breakfast."

I started to say something and noticed my phone buzzed indicating a call from Lauren. "Sendy, guess who's calling me?"

"Lauren?" She laughed.

"Yes."

"Well, I'll let you go, dear. Pray the interview goes well. Running a B&B is something Candace and Caleb have always wanted to do. Love ya."

"Love ya, too." I switched over to Lauren's call.

"Lauren Treavor, how are you doing?"

"Sis, you're not going to believe what I just found out."

I didn't say a word.

"Mick's going to talk to Sendy's son and daughter-in-law about running his grandma's bed and breakfast!"

"That's absolutely fantastic." I walked onto the porch of cottage one. "I have to be honest…"

"Are you okay? The babies?"

I sat on the porch swing and put it in motion. "We're okay. Sendy called me right before you did."

"Guess she's as excited as Mick and me. I hope it works out with Caleb and Candace since they don't live that far from the ranch. Please pray, Sis."

"Let's do it right now." I cleared my throat. "Lord, we thank You for Caleb and Candace and are so grateful You placed them in Wyoming. We ask that this interview goes as well as possible for all concerned. But more importantly, Your will be done. Thank You, Jesus. Amen."

"Thanks, Sis. Renovations begin the end of this week regardless of anyone running the B&B."

"Lauren, after looking at all the pictures you sent of the bed and breakfast, I have tons of affordable ideas. No walls need to come down, just interior design. I'll send you my thoughts after our call. Okay?"

"Sure." She sniffled. "A couple other things have happened, too."

"What?"

"You know how frail Ike Woods is. Mick's mom gets Penelope ready for school each morning and to bed each evening. I didn't know about it until we came to Wyoming, and she shared that with me. I need your honest opinion."

"Lauren Wyatt Treavor, when haven't I been honest with you?"

"Never."

"Tell me what's going on, please. Before I burst!"

"When Mick and I return to Hope, I'm contemplating helping with Penny. I'll have a lot of juggling to do. What do you think? Am I being ridiculous to think I can manage babysitting, marriage, and helping with school and the rec building?" She snuffled. "I look at everything you manage and here I am whining."

"You want to know my opinion, so here goes. For one thing you are not whining. For another thing, I think it's monumental."

"Monumental? Where did that word come from?" she razzed.

"I don't know, but I'm sure the definition is something magnificent. You know, Sis, I remember at one point in time you said you didn't think you'd get a puppy. Look at you, the mother of Heidi dog."

"What does that have to do with watching a little girl, teaching, and other stuff?"

"It has a lot to do with it. You're giving love and time to Heidi just like you'll find the time to give help to Penelope, Mr. Wood, and your mom-in-law. That's so selfless. I believe you'll do great with all the tasks at hand. And you do know, I'll be on call for anything you need." I took a deep breath. "By the way, what does Mick think?"

"He reminded me we're a team, and I'm not alone. We'll stand hand in hand with God in the lead." She paused. "I'm just a bag of emotions, Rae, and it's not hormones!"

"Oh, Lauren, that 'h' word drives me loony. I'm so excited for you and Mick. You know what, if you need help with Penny when you get back, Joe and I will watch her so you and Mick can have an official honeymoon."

"That would really be nice. You're the best!"

"On another note, I'll check on your house tomorrow."

"The crew sends pictures every day and it looks wonderful. I'll need your decorating expertise when we get to that point, but first I want ideas for the Wyoming bed and breakfast. By the way, the interview with Caleb and Candace is tomorrow morning."

"I can't wait to hear all about it."

"I'll let you know."

"Joe and I are thinking about having another town hall meeting right after July 4th. Speaking of which, another hysterical society meeting is scheduled for next Monday. I haven't looked up Plan 2D, but I will before we meet. From what I hear the ladies have everything under control. I'm excited about my first Independence Day here."

"Are you sure Grace is leaving the planning in y'all's hands? Better check with the Greenville-Spartanburg airport and see if she's reserved a helicopter to fly over the lake."

"Fly over the lake? What are you talking about, silly girl?"

Lauren giggled. "Maybe she'll toss sparklers out of the flying contraption on July 4th, since there won't be any fireworks."

"Haha. You rascal." I paused. "Wait a minute, that's actually a great idea!"

"A helicopter?"

"No. The sparklers. I'll check with the society to find out if we can commandeer enough sparklers for everyone to use. Maybe we could ride the paddle boats and canoes on the lake with them in our hands. They might've done that before since you and I have never been here for the fourth, but it's worth asking."

"Rae, you could send an e-mail to the ladies and find out. Just a thought since I'm not an official member." She mumbled something under her breath.

"Did I just hear you say 'thankfully' when you mentioned you're not an official member of the society?"

"No worries about your hearing, Mrs. Byer. I thought I was discreet," she teased.

"You know what? I'll send the e-mail now while we're talking. I'm forwarding a courtesy copy to you since you'll be inducted when you return home."

"Thanks. Well, I'll let you go. I know you're busy getting ready for guests."

"I don't want to complain, but Martha Ingle's mom and dad are arriving this afternoon."

"Nothing more needs to be said," she groaned. "I love you and Joe. Hug Heidi for me. I miss that sweet puppy of mine."

"Love you, Sis. Bye."

* * *

I sent the e-mail to all the society members and quickly got responses. They'd never done the sparkler idea because they always had fireworks. They loved the suggestion.

I noticed an e-mail from Grace to all the members:

Girls. Brilliant idea. Fran's husband, George, oversees the fireworks. Let him know the idea. Tata for now.

Victoria responded to all of us. "Rae is brilliant. We never would have thought of it if it hadn't been for her."

Quick response from me. "Actually, Lauren thought of the sparklers."

Thumbs up from all the members. Including Grace.

You are bringing some strange ideas to our
ears... Acts 17:20

Chapter 32

Text from Martha Ingles.

Martha: Mom and Dad running late. Be there around 5

Me: No worries. We're ready

Martha: You sure? LOL

Me: Thumbs up and smiley face emoji

I noticed another message.

Joe: Mind setting up meeting with Yvette and Anne? I'd mentioned meeting this week when we had the town hall.

Me: I'll set it for Thurs. BTW: Chandlers here soon. I'm stressed. Hope they won't occupy my time.

Joe: No problem. They can come to mtng.

Me: You're kidding, right?

Joe: Kissing face emoji

I messaged Yvette and Anne with a Thursday night dinner invite at the Inn for them and their hubbies. They accepted without spouses. Dr. D and Anne's husband had board meetings at the university that evening.

I immediately texted Joe.

Me: Are you going to the mtng Thurs night?

Joe: Uh-oh. I am.

Me: I'll meet with them.

Joe: Sounds good.

I strolled to the front porch with my broom in hand. I was thrilled to see a fluorescent box decorated with pipe cleaners, stickers, and glitter. A note fluttered on top. "Rae, this is it! Hope the box works for the names!" Fran.

I immediately texted my dear friend to thank her, then sent an e-mail to all Hope residents informing them the drop box was on the premises and ready for suggestions.

* * *

The Chandler's sparkly new SUV pulled in front of cottage four as I waited at the door.

Mr. Chandler opened the door and waved. "Hey, Rae. Good to see you again. Sorry we're late."

"So good to see you, Sir. You're not late at all." I descended the porch steps toward Mrs. Chandler's car door. Before my hand reached the handle, I noticed her sitting inside with arms folded across her ample chest.

Mr. Chandler scuttled to my side. "Mrs. Byer, no need to help. Mrs. Chandler needs a little extra assistance these days. I need to get a step stool out of the back." He opened the passenger door and slowly pulled out a hefty metal footstool.

I moved back onto the porch, didn't say a word, and observed as Mr. Chandler maneuvered the steps into position and opened the passenger door.

Mrs. Chandler unfolded her arms and squirmed her way onto the steps, straightened her gingham mumu, then shuffled toward the cottage. "Well, Rae, I'm glad to see you shored up the handrails for the steps. Last time I almost fell."

I cleared my throat, pulled a tissue from my pocket, and wiped my brow. "It's so good to see you." I opened the door to the cottage then stepped aside. "Do y'all need any help with your luggage?"

Mr. Chandler shook his head. "Little lady, there's no way you're carrying Mrs. C's bags. You're expecting and are already carrying enough."

Mrs. C glowered at him and stepped inside.

Joe had hired Nathaniel for summer help so I sent the teenager a quick text.

Me: Need help at cottage 4 ASAP!

Nathaniel: At land. On way

"Mr. Chandler, please leave your items in the car. Nathaniel will help."

"I like that idea." He took one step at a time, reached the porch, then turned my way. "We appreciate your hospitality."

No sooner had he finished his comment when Nathaniel arrived in the golf cart. "Mrs. Byer, where should I put the suitcases?"

Mr. Chandler inserted, "Nathaniel, follow me. Let's ask Mrs. Chandler. She's inside the cabin and knows what's best."

My sixteen-year-old hire responded with confidence. "Yes, Sir."

Mr. C looked at Nathaniel. "Well, young man, you have a bright future ahead of you." The elderly man led the way inside the cottage.

I waited outside for Nathaniel to return. He stepped out the door and strutted to where I stood. "Mr. Chandler gave me a tip. I told him he didn't have to." He chuckled. "His wife kept telling me where to put the suitcases, then changed her mind three times. He said I more than earned it." He pushed his glasses up on his nose. "I can put up with people changing their minds if I get this kind of money." He grinned.

"Keep up the good work, Nathaniel. Thanks for your help." *I hope that's the only thing Mrs. C changes while here.*

* * *

I scuttled to the Inn and peeked inside the box on the front porch. Several folded papers covered the bottom of the cardboard. I chuckled to myself then trudged upstairs. Just as I sat down, the dogs started barking incessantly. "Shush! What in the world are you barking at?" I peeked out of our second-floor bedroom window to see why they were going berserk.

An F-250 diesel with a horse trailer attached parked in front of the Inn. *What in the world?*

"Come on dogs, we're checking this out." I opened the upstairs door and the four of them bolted downstairs with hackles maxed and me at their heels. I pushed open the front doors and halted in my tracks.

Quinn opened the truck door, unfolded himself from the front seat, then tipped his cowboy hat at me. "Hey, Rae. Surprised?"

"Very."

"I decided to bring a few of my horses. Long ride from Texas."

"Where's Sendy?" I squirmed. "Thought y'all were returning on Friday."

"She's flying here Friday cuz she didn't want to travel in the truck."

I don't blame her. "Where are the horses staying?"

"Boarding them at Val's. The corral is done next week."

"Okay."

"I'm not building stalls on the land. I'm paying Val to board them in her barn. It's a win-win for us both." He peeled off his hat and tossed it into the front seat. "I had lots of time to think on the trip. We don't need another meeting with the town folk now since it'll be a while till the rec building is done." He stretched his arms above his head. "Doggone arthritis."

"Uncle Quinn, do you need a cottage?"

"Nope. I'm doing some carpentry work for Grace and Lance while they're on their trip and will stay at their place. When Sendy comes back here, we'll get our old cottage back." He leveraged himself back into the truck cab. "I have a few horses to tend to. See you Friday." He revved his engine and pulled the rig around the circular driveway.

That man never ceased to amaze me.

* * *

I noticed a missed text.

Yvette: Call me pls. Not urgent

I snatched a cold-water bottle from the fridge, then moseyed outside to the front porch swing. "Yvette, everything okay?"

"Anne and I have a conflict with Thursday evening. We forgot about a speaking engagement at the art museum in Greenville that night. We're embarrassed to say it's been on our calendars for a month."

"No worries at all. What are you gals doing now?"

"We're heading to Bitty's Buns in a few." She paused. "Wanna join us?"

"I'd love too. Would y'all have time to go over plans for the art studio?"

"That'd be perfect. We've already met with each other about the building, so can't wait to share our ideas with you."

"See ya."

* * *

I sauntered upstairs to freshen up, then sent a text to Joe explaining about the meeting.

After twisting my mane into a Dutch braid, slipping into a hot pink sun dress, and putting on flip flops, I opted to drive my VW convertible with the top down.

Anne and Yvette waved as I parked near an outdoor table with a striped umbrella.

"Hey girls! So glad this worked out for the three of us."

"We are, too."

Anne took me by the arm. "Now come on, little mama. You need to get inside and cool off a bit."

I laughed then sashayed inside with the two artists.

Natalie escorted us to the back of the tiny bakery. "You gals talking about the art studio?"

"We are."

"It'll be magnificent. Something we've needed for a long time in this little town." She straightened her powder pink apron. "What can I get y'all?"

Anne and Yvette ordered large, sweet teas with lemon meringue pie. I opted for a glass of milk and coconut cream pie.

Yvette set her portfolio on a nearby chair. "These are our ideas. Let's eat first then get down to business."

I subdued a giggle. These ladies were professionals and I loved it.

A few minutes later, Natalie and her daughter, Hannah, placed our delectable desserts in front of us.

I took a sip of my milk, "Hannah, good to see you. We'll need to schedule a meeting with you and Shelly soon to set up the dance and music building. By the way, is Peaches and Cream closed today?"

Hannah stood straight as an arrow as only a ballerina can do. "The owner's cleaning crew is there for a few days, so no work for Sidney and me. But we still get paid." She sniggled.

Natalie tapped her daughter on the shoulder. "Enough about that, young lady. We have more customers to serve." She glared at Hannah, then turned to wink at us.

* * *

Hannah refilled our glasses then returned to our table with our checks. "Thank you for coming ladies. Hope to see you again soon." She grinned.

I motioned at Hannah. "You know what? If you have any free time before you go back to Peaches and Cream, maybe we can coordinate with Shelly about the dance studio this week."

Hannah beamed. "That'd be great!"

"I'll check with Shelly and you check with your mother, then we can come up with a date and plan." I heard Hannah whistling as she practically pranced back to the counter.

Natalie discreetly crept our way and muttered. "I couldn't help but hear what you said to Hannah. That girl has been beside herself with joy at the prospect of helping Shelly. I can let her skip a few hours from work here to discuss the plans for the project any time you suggest." She attempted a pirouette, caught herself mid-spin, then returned to the front of the bakery.

Anne placed the layout to the building on a table, while Yvette put color, floor, countertop, and wall samples on another.

"You two are awesome. Please tell me your ideas."

Yvette wiped her forehead with her napkin. "I swanny, girls, I'm as nervous as a porcupine in a balloon factory."

Anne rolled her eyes. "Yvette, there's no need to worry. You've got this, girl. Tell Rae where everything's going in the building so I can explain the color palette and other ideas."

I roared with laughter. "You gals are funny. I'm ready to hear and see everything."

Yvette pointed to different areas on the design. "You notice, we have a designated area for pottery and will have a potter's wheel. I did a little research on my own and found out an old high school in Greenville closed and has a potter's wheel we can have for free if we haul it off." She sipped her drink. "What do you think?"

"I'm ecstatic! I love the idea."

Yvette grinned and then proceeded. "Cleanup will be easy. One wall will be nothing but windows. The lighting will be perfect for painting or any other creative activity that we want. One more thing. I have tons of supplies we can use for classes. My hubby will be more than pleased for me to get rid of the stuff. It's filling up the garage. Any questions, Rae?"

"I'm thrilled with your ideas. Only question I have is when can we get started?"

"When you agree to everything and give my husband, also known as Doodles, the go- ahead." She twittered.

Anne cleared her throat. "I've chosen a turquoise palette. Of course, pops of color and texture will be throughout the building. After all, it is an art studio, isn't it girls?" She didn't wait for an answer. "We've chosen very durable laminate flooring, floor to ceiling storage on the wall opposite the windows, and the counters will be stainless. And guess what?" She kept talking. "The school that's being torn down in Greenville has shelving. I saw the shelves on line and some of them are worn and a little junky looking, but we can master that. Best part is they're free if we transport them. I'll check the website again to see if they have tables, chairs, and things like that. Once we get all that finalized, we can get started. Oh, I could go on and on. So, what do you think, Rae? Any questions?"

"You've made it all very clear and I love the ideas. I can't wait for y'all to get started. As far as I'm concerned, it's a go, but let me take a few pictures, send them to Quinn, Sendy, and Joe, and get their okay. I'll let y'all know their opinions." I took photos and sent them before Anne and Yvette put the samples into a large cloth bag.

Natalie stood with her hands propped on her hips. "If I get a vote, I say your ideas are fabulous!"

My phone buzzed and within seconds I received answers from everyone. "Thumbs up."

"We are all in agreement and Natalie has given the final approval." I giggled and announced. "Your plans and design are perfect. They can be submitted to Dr. Duntworth and his crew. I'll send pictures to the Historical Ladies and Lauren, too."

Anne laughed. "Better hurry or Grace will send them first."

The three of us laughed in unison.

At the present time your plenty will supply
what they need... 2 Corinthians 8:14

Chapter 33

Two more couples arrived the day after the Chandler's. Cottages were assigned to each, and Molly arrived early a.m. to start breakfast. The scent of homemade waffles and bacon permeated the entire Inn.

I followed my nose down the stairs and toward the kitchen. "Molly, how can I help?"

"What are you doing up so early, dear?" She glanced at her watch. "Six-thirty? Babies' wake you?"

"The smell of your waffles and bacon did." I hugged her waist. "How are you feeling?"

"Surgery is scheduled July 5th and I'm more than ready. In the meantime, I need to take these to the Chandlers." She winked, snatched a tray with two covered waffle and bacon filled plates, then paused. "Forgot the silverware. Mrs. C likes plastic utensils. Says the metal ones hurt her teeth."

"Her false teeth?" I covered my mouth with my hand and mumbled. "Shame on me."

Molly set the tray down and almost doubled over with laughter. "Yes, shame on you, dear." She winked then picked up the shabby sheek tray.

"Wait a sec. I didn't see the Chandlers in the dining area when I came downstairs."

"That's because I'm delivering breakfast to their bungalow."

I patted her hand and took the tray from Chef Molly. "I'll take it to them. You have enough to do before the other couples' traipse in to eat." I picked up the tray and toddled toward the front doors. Fortunately, my timing was perfect because guests arrived and held them open for me. "Welcome y'all. I'll be back in a minute. Please seat yourselves." I beamed.

* * *

Mr. Chandler greeted me on the porch. "Thanks so much, Rae. I know room service isn't your usual routine, but Mrs. Chandler didn't rest well last night and is still in her gown. I love eating in the dining room so I can fill up on the buffet."

"Mr. Chandler, I'll gladly get you more if you just send me a text. How are you doing?"

His wife shouted for him to come inside. "Mrs. Byer, I'll take that." He took the tray from me. "Thank you."

"If you need anything else let us know." I gently patted his shoulder.

"Martha is taking us to lunch and then--." His wife groaned from inside the cottage. "Better go."

Please be with Mr. Chandler, Lord.

* * *

I stepped onto the Inn porch, peeked inside the decorated box, and noticed it was half full of folded pieces of paper. *I need to tell folks we'll stop taking suggestions in a couple days.* The chatter inside the Inn's dining room lured me in. Two couples sat at the harvest table. I stopped near the buffet and waited for a pause in their conversation. "We're so glad you're here. Where are y'all from?"

They all said in unison, "Beaufort."

One of the men added, "We're on my brother, Earnie's, team and will finish the splash pad by next week. He hired all of us. So here we are." He motioned at the other people sitting nearby.

A petite brunette laughed. "Collette told us this town is adorable and everyone is so friendly. I swanny she was right. Reminds us of Beaufort only without the Bay." She slid a piece of bacon off her plate. "Have you been to Beaufort?"

I removed a water pitcher from the sideboard and proceeded to refill their glasses. "I've never been there but would love to visit. I helped prepare a Low Country boil, though."

Earnie's brother teased, "Well then, you're a true Beaufortonian."

I laughed then slipped into the kitchen.

* * *

With everyone settled, I walked downtown with water bottle in tow. The cloudy sky and slight breeze drew me to my favorite bench across from the lake. I flopped onto the spot where Joe had proposed to me. I loved that memory. I closed my eyes, tilted my head back to face the sky, and almost fell asleep till a light flutter from a low branch swished above me. My mind darted to a time not too long ago when I told Joe we were having a baby and he surprised me. He already knew.

The babies moved in my tummy and brought me back to reality. *Think I'll stop at Sweetness and Sweaters to check on Lauren's mom.*

* * *

As I slid off the bench and headed toward the little shop, I heard my name being shouted.

"Rae, Rae."

I halted in my tracks and turned in the direction of my name. "Martha?"

"I went by the Inn and noticed the sign saying you were out." She scampered in my direction. "I'm glad I tracked you down. I wanted to talk to you with my parents out of earshot."

"Are you okay? Your parents?" I wiped beads of perspiration off my forehead.

"Do you have time to go to Molly's?"

"I sure do." *I hope Martha's mother isn't complaining about the Bed and Breakfast.*

* * *

We entered Molly's Restaurant, Henry greeted us, then escorted us to a booth near the back of the diner. "What can I get you ladies?"

Martha blurted, "Lemonade and cherry pie." She grinned.

"I'll have lemonade and blueberry pie."

"Got it. Martha, how are your mom and dad? I heard they're here for a visit."

"They're doing as well as possible. Thanks for asking, Henry."

"Glad to hear it." He trudged toward the kitchen.

Martha took a deep breath then proceeded. "Rae, my mother and father love Hope." She paused.

"That's wonderful."

"As you know, my mom is quite opinionated."

I didn't say a word and folded my hands on the table.

"They're leaving Anderson and moving here."

"When?"

"Next month."

"Where will they live?" I fiddled with my earring.

"Mom wants to live with my hubby, the kids, and me."

"Oh, my."

Henry arrived with our sugary delights then turned toward other tables and customers.

I took a gulp of lemonade. "Martha, do you need help with anything?" I took a bite of my pie.

"I don't know. My dad thinks they should live independently."

"Have you spoken to Mick. You know he's the best realtor there is. I don't say that just because he's married to Lauren."

"I thought about it, but he's not in town."

"That doesn't matter. He has access to a computer even while in Wyoming."

She chuckled. "You're right. I'll call him tomorrow. Or maybe today." She drummed her fingers on the table. "I might as well ask this. Mom and dad want to know if they can rent a cottage for the next month."

I choked on a crumb then took a tiny sip of my drink. "They what?"

Martha patted my hand. "It's not my idea, Rae. I think they should stay in their home in Anderson for the next month." She pulled her phone from her purse. "I'll call Mick now if you don't mind."

I gave her a thumbs up.

She made the call while I excused myself and chatted with Henry at the counter. In a short while Martha waved my way for me to return.

I slipped onto the chair and sat on the edge of the seat. "Everything okay?"

"Mick said he has three listings that might work, but even if my folks decide on one, it'll take a while for the closing. I can't imagine them living with me." She palmed her forehead, took a gulp of her drink, then speed talked through the rest of her explanation. "I have an appointment for my parent's and me tomorrow morning at Tweeters Realty. Since Mick won't be there in person, he's having Jamie help us. He'll walk us through the whole thing via Facetime if we need it." She ate the last morsel of pie, grabbed her purse, and pushed out of her chair. "Better tell Mom and Dad."

She practically floated out the restaurant door.

I still don't know if the Chandlers will need a cottage for a month.

Therefore do not worry about tomorrow, for
tomorrow will worry about itself...
Matthew 6:34

Chapter 34

I decided to skip a visit to Sweetness and Sweaters and moseyed back to the Inn just in time to meet Joe on the front porch. "Hey, Beautiful. I just noticed your note on the door." He bent down and peered inside the suggestion box. "Wow this thing's almost full."

"I've been gone most of the afternoon. I sent an e-mail to the masses that tomorrow will be our last day to take suggestions for the name of the recreation area." I folded my hands on my middle. "You're never going to believe who's moving to Hope."

"Who?"

"Let's go inside."

He mumbled, "Everything all right?"

I practically shoved him inside and into the four massive hounds that greeted us with their tails swinging.

He scratched the first furry head to reach him. "Rae, what's going on?"

"I'll let the dogs outside first." I opened the back door, and they dashed outside. I joined him in the kitchen.

He plopped his backpack on the island, grabbed two glasses from the cupboard, filled them with ice water, then handed me one. "Are you okay?"

"The Chandler's are moving here."

"Martha's folks?"

"Uh-huh. They're thinking about renting a cottage for a month, but I suggested Martha talk to Mick so they can move into a house..."

"Take a breath, Rae." He kissed my forehead. "Let me get this straight. They're moving here, but don't have a place to live?"

"That's right. Martha doesn't really want her folks living with her." I took a breath. "She called Mick and he has a few places her folks can look at, but it'll take a while to close the deal even if they pick one quickly."

"Tell ya what. I'll change out of this suit and take you to supper. Then we can discuss this in detail. Maybe if the Chandlers stay at the Inn, it'll work out for Martha." He opened the door for P, B, T, and H, filled their bowls with kibble and cool water, then took my hand as we strolled upstairs. "Wanna go to Gill's?"

"I like that idea." *But I don't like the idea of them staying at the Inn.*

* * *

We ordered our usual at Gill's and the loud music kept our discussion discreet.

"Joe, I'll go crazy if the Chandlers stay at the Inn for a month. And what if it's even longer?" I sipped an ice filled glass of apple juice.

"Let's take it one day at a time."

"Easy peasy for you to say. I'll be dealing with them constantly, Professor." I cringed.

"You're right, but you won't be alone, Beautiful."

The jukebox played our song, *"Everything"*, and Joe took my hand and led me to the crowded dance floor. "One step at a time, Gorgeous."

"Joseph, I feel huge. How can I be gorgeous?"

No explanation needed as he held me close and nuzzled my neck.

The song ended, he paid the bill, and we headed home in his clunky truck.

My phone buzzed as Joe parked his Ford. "I hope it's not the Chandlers." I snatched the phone from my purse. "It's Lauren." I immediately pressed the button to take the call. "How are you—?"

Lauren interrupted. "I'm doing great. Wait a minute, I hear music in the background. Where are you?"

"Joe and I and are in his truck and the radio's blaring. Mind if I put you on speaker?" I turned down the music.

"Sendy's son and daughter-in-law will manage Grandma Alana's property. The interview went perfectly!"

"Congrats, Lauren!"

"Thanks for praying. One more thing. Heard Chandlers are thinking about staying in a cottage for a month. No worries, Sis. Mick will do his best to find them something quickly. Better run. Construction work is about to end here for the day, so Mick and I are going out to celebrate. Love you both."

"Love to y'all, too."

* * *

Joe delivered a small burlap bag filled with a bottle of sparkling cider, warm mixed nuts, and two apples to each cottage while I showered and slipped into my seersucker gown. I crawled under clean sheets and nestled into my pillow. Slumber came quickly. So quickly I never knew when Joe and our pups went to sleep near me.

My people will live in peaceful dwelling places...
Isaiah 32:18

Chapter 35

My thick mane tangled and twisted into knots. I'd gone to bed the night before without drying and braiding my hair like I usually did. I snatched a large hairclip off the bathroom sink, clipped my hair into a very messy do, then readied for the day. My pale blue linen flouncy dress would wrinkle like crazy, but I didn't care. Linen made me feel cool, and that's all that mattered. I added several of my mother's bangles to my wrist, then clipped antique baubles to my lobes. With flip flops on my tootsies, I ambled downstairs and into the kitchen.

"Molly, how are you?" I hugged her waist.

"Good, sweet girl." She slid a few plates into the dishwasher. "All the Beaufort folks have gone to work on the splash pad. Martha sent me a text that her folks won't be here for breakfast because she's taking them to my restaurant this morning." She wiped the counter.

"Did you know they're moving here?"

"I heard through the grapevine. Martha used to practically beg them to move here and quit asking several years ago."

"What do you mean?"

"Mrs. Chandler refused. She can be pretty stubborn. Bless her heart."

"You're so right. Don't know if you've heard the Chandlers might stay in a cottage for a month." I rolled my eyes.

Molly handed me a glass of milk and chuckled. "I did hear that info, but didn't want to give you indigestion this morning.

Did you know Mrs. Chandler is a Master Gardener. She used to be so much fun."

"I can't picture Mrs. C working in a yard. What happened?"

"I'm not sure. All I know is sweet Martha thinks her mother needs a purpose."

I pulled an orange-cranberry scone from the covered cake plate. "I don't want to cause trouble especially if Mrs. C stays at the Inn longer, but I wonder if there's something she could do at the new property?"

Molly poured herself a cup of java and snatched a blueberry muffin from a sealed container. "Rae, I think you might've come up with an idea."

I paused. "Maybe she could help choose plants to surround the small buildings. We hired a landscaper to design the larger areas surrounding the gravel pathways and parking area. What do you think?"

"Maybe you'd better check with your hubby, first."

"You're right."

* * *

Joe got home from work, and we opted to go to Molly's Restaurant for supper. Red gardenias in large white pots dotted each step to the red, white, and blue ribboned wreath on the entryway door. So patriotic.

As we walked inside, I chuckled at the sight of red and white twinkle lights draped from each corner of the ceiling and paper fireworks taped to the walls.

I whispered, "Ya think it's almost Independence Day, Joe?"

He squeezed my hand. "I'm not sure." Crooked grin.

Sidney greeted us and led us to our usual booth. "Hey, y'all. What can I get you to drink?"

I grinned. "My usual, please."

Sidney blushed. "Pregnancy usual or non-pregnancy usual?"

"Oh, Sidney. I know it's not obvious that I'm expecting." I sniggled.

We told her we wanted the special for dinner. No sooner had we ordered, Emily and Blake entered the restaurant and threaded through tables to our booth.

Emily stood with a hand on her baby bump. "Mind if we join, y'all? I hear the Chandlers might be staying at the Inn for a long time." She blurted.

Blake interjected, "Honey, maybe they're having a romantic dinner."

Joe laughed. "Not hardly."

Emily and her hubby scooched onto the bench seat across from us. "Rae is the info true? Mom called me today and asked about the Chandlers."

I almost choked on my water. "I can't believe your mom found out." I tapped my finger on my temple. "Of course, small town and Historical Society informants!"

Joe laughed. "Em, it's true that they might stay at the cottages. Nothing's confirmed just yet. We'll send a community wide e-mail when we find out."

I jokingly punched Joe on the arm. "Good one, hubby."

Emily started to spout off something to her brother but instead waved toward the doorway. "We need to push some tables together because there's a big crowd coming."

Earnest, Collette, and the splash pad crew paraded inside behind Henry. He attempted to shove tables together until Joe, Blake, and the workers took over.

Collette balanced her daughter on her hip and stepped in our direction. "Hey, Girls."

I slid from the booth and reached for Daisy. "Mind if I hold her?"

Collette giggled. "Are you offering to hold her through dinner?" She laughed.

"Absolutely."

"I was only kidding. But you can hold her for a few minutes." She handed her daughter to me.

Emily squirmed. "I want a turn, too."

I cradled the sweet baby, then passed her to my sis-in-law. Collette sat in our booth while Joe and Blake joined the workers at the makeshift community table.

I glanced at the two female crew members drumming their fingers on the table. "Mind if I ask them to join us?"

Collette spoke softly. "That would be great. They work for Earnest and are part of the crew and we never get a chance to visit. As weird as this sounds, sometimes it's hard being the boss's wife."

I walked to their table, invited them to join us, and they accepted. "Hope we didn't take you from an important business discussion."

One of the ladies shook her head. "You saved us from boredom. I think I can speak for the two of us." She looked at the other wife who grinned.

With introductions made, they ordered the special. Daisy sat comfortably in a wooden highchair as we all chatted and enjoyed the spaghetti, house salad with homemade croutons, and garlic bread. No romantic meals with our hubbies. Crazy laughter with women who needed this getaway time. No men allowed!

* * *

Our fur babies greeted us when we opened the front doors and followed us through the foyer and out the back door.

I grabbed a ball off the chaise lounge and threw it to them. Buddy retrieved it while the other three dogs chased him. "Good job, sweet pups." I fluffed their gargantuan ears then turned to Joe. "Want your ears fluffed, too, Mr. Byer?"

"No. I wouldn't mind a kiss, though." He strutted my way, squeezed between the dogs and me, and planted a lingering kiss on my lips. "Now, that's more like it."

"Much better than ear fluffing." I laughed.

"You bet."

He filled the doggy bowls with cold water and added water to our birdbath. "Thanks, Husband. Do you mind if I go back inside? I need to call Shelly and set up a date for her and Hannah to meet with me about the dance/music building."

"Nope. While you're doing that, I'll take the dogs on a walk to the land."

"Great idea."

* * *

"Shelly, this is Rae. How are you doing?"

"Just fine. And you?"

"Fine. I wanted to know if you can meet tomorrow to discuss the dance studio." I paused. "I'm so sorry this is last minute."

"You know what? That'll be perfect. Emily's taking the kiddos to the movie. I don't want her to overdo it, and she assured me an air-conditioned theater and popcorn are exactly what she needs. I believe she's just being sweet."

"I can tell you for a fact, Emily loves working for you and Javier."

"She's part of our family. Now back to business." She giggled. "What time and where do you want to meet?"

"How about three tomorrow. Hannah will be between shifts at Molly's Restaurant, and I'm assuming you're not as busy at Fenster Haus at that time. I guess I shouldn't assume."

"That's a great time. Let's meet at the studio."

"I love that idea. Shall I bring my toe shoes?" I sniggled. "Not!"

"See you tomorrow." She laughed.

* * *

I snuggled next to my hubby with four canines at our feet. "Joseph, know what? I found out Martha's mom is a Master Gardener."

He yawned. "Okay."

"She really is. I was thinking about asking her to pick the plants and flowers to go around the two designated buildings on the land."

He propped himself on one elbow and looked me in the eyes. "I'm not sure I heard you right. You want Mrs. Chandler, the lady who always complains, to help with the land? Why?"

"Molly and I were brainstorming. She mentioned Mrs. Chandler used to be a funny person and likes working with flowers and plants."

"Wife of mine, if she stays here for a long time and works in the garden you might really stress."

"I know. I just thought it might help Martha and maybe her dad, too."

"Let's pray about it. If anything, talk to Martha before you make any decisions." He took my hands in his. "I must admit, you and the babies are my priority." He prayed, kissed my cheek, turned over, and within seconds fell fast asleep.

Good advice, Handsome. Night, night, Joseph William Byer. I love you more than you'll ever know.

If any of you lacks wisdom, you should ask
God... James 1:5

Chapter 36

My phone buzzed. E-mail to all the Historical Society ladies from the President, aka, my mother-in-law, Grace:

Fran's husband, George, called me early this morning. I'm so sorry to let y'all know, Fran had a miscarriage last night and is in the hospital. She's having a few complications. George needs help with the children. I'll do whatever I can from here since I'm still not home in Hope. Pray.

Responses came from every member. It was decided. Victoria went to Fran's home to stay with the children. Anne and Lottie would pick up meals from Molly's Restaurant to take to Fran's home. Emily and I would help at Fran's flower shop.

I called my sister-in-law. "Emily, it's so sad to hear about the baby."

"My heart's broken. I guess I take it for granted that my baby is growing inside me." She sniffled.

"I do, too. You and I are so fortunate." I wiped my nose. "Molly is here at the Inn and making breakfast for everyone, so I can be at Buds and Blooms in about thirty minutes. I don't know much about plants and flowers."

"Me either. I'll be there in thirty minutes, too."

I ended one call and noticed another from my mother-in-law. "Grace?"

"Rae, I know you and Emily will help at Fran's flower shop. You might not know this. Pearl is a Master Gardener and knows everything about plants and flowers. I've asked her to help you and Emily at Buds and Blooms."

I thought for a second, "Is Pearl Mrs. Chandler?"

"Of course."

"I didn't know her first name."

"She'll start at the shop tomorrow. By the way, I already told Emily that Lance and I'll be home in a few days. No use staying gone longer. The town needs me...us. Don't overdo it. Bye."

* * *

I cruised in my VW Bug down Beaufort Street and parked in front of Buds and Blooms. Emily's Mini pulled into the spot next to mine. We found the hidden spare key inside a plastic container in the window box and let ourselves inside.

I gulped. "Em, this is so weird. I hope Fran's okay."

"Me, too."

We inched through the tiny shop, and I noticed a legal pad on the counter. "Look at this. It's an itemized list of customers and their orders."

Emily thumbed through the pages. "Mrs. Chandler better get here fast because I know nothing about this."

"It's just you and me today." Fran's meticulous attention to detail was mind boggling. Each refrigerated flower container had the name of the flowers that were inside. "We can do this for Fran and her family."

"You know Mom and Daddy are coming home in a few days."

I grabbed a glass vase off the shelf. "Yep. Now, let's get to work."

"Sounds good." She picked the flowers that's names were written on the paper, completed the first task, and started on the next.

The shop door opened and in walked Anne. "Hey, girls, there just aren't words in this situation. Yvette's waiting in her truck for the flowers we need to deliver today." She picked up two arrangements we'd put in a box. "That's the least we can do."

I opened the front door, waved to Yvette, and watched as Anne shoved the cardboard box into the bed of the truck.

Emily stood near the back of the shop. As I walked a little closer to where she was, I heard her whimpering. "Rae, I complain about my swollen feet, my hair, my belly. I hurt for Fran and George. I can't imagine losing this little baby." She patted her baby bump.

I hugged my sis-in-law. "You know what? I whimper and whine about pregnancy stuff, too, Let's make a pact. No more griping. Let's focus on how we can help them."

The two of us hustled to finish the rest of the projects. At noon the shop bell above the door jingled and I looked up to see my hubby.

He weaved through the refrigerated display cases and hugged me gently. "Sorry I didn't get here sooner." He kissed my neck.

"I knew you were in meetings, Professor. You didn't need to come, but I'm glad you did."

"I'm glad I did, too." He hugged me gently, then glanced at his sister. "Emily, I told Blake I'd check on you. He's in class now." He moved closer to his sister and gave her a hug.

"Thanks, big brother." She hugged him back then threw clippings into a container.

"Can I get you ladies something to eat? It's about lunchtime."

"Handsome, I'd love a chicken wrap from Bitty's Buns and lemonade."

Emily piped up, "I'll have the same, please."

Joe headed to Natalie's restaurant and returned shortly with our lunch. "Here, girls. Natalie threw in fruit tarts for dessert." He set the two powder blue bags on the counter with our lemonades beside them. "I better get back to work. Don't overdo it." He hugged my bulging middle, kissed my lips, then told us goodbye.

We enjoyed our lunch at the counter. The morning orders were done and delivered so we had a few minutes to relax.

"Emily, I just remembered I have a meeting this afternoon with Shelly and Hannah. I better let them know I need to cancel."

"Why should you cancel?" she pointed at Fran's legal pad. "There's nothing on the list for this afternoon. I'll write on the white board that we're closed for the day and will return tomorrow. What do ya think?"

"I think it's a great idea. You're welcome to join us for the meeting."

"Don't think so. I don't feel much like a ballerina right now with this bulging baby bump." She placed her hand over her mouth. "Oops! I said I wouldn't complain."

We finished our meal, straightened the shop, and tossed clippings into the compost container near the back picket fence.

"Rae, I'm going to Angels to Zithers to check on my mom-in-law. Tilly's still helping while Sea's gone." She hugged my neck. "I hope tomorrow goes as smoothly when Mrs. Chandler is here." She rolled her eyes.

"Oh, you mean Pearl?" I winked.

"Is that her first name?"

"Yes."

"I never knew." Emily laughed.

* * *

I puttered home in my Bug, made a beeline into the powder room, and heard my precious hound dogs whining outside the door. "Be there in a minute." When I opened the door, their tails whipped back and forth, and I couldn't resist a kiss on their noses. "Come on. I know you need a powder room visit, too." I let them outside, snatched three water bottles from the fridge, and halted. It dawned on me I'd never spoken to Kelly about her ideas for the music area, so I sent her a text.

Me: Mtng with Shelly and Hannah today--can you join online? Sorry last minute.

I let my sweet fur babies inside, watered the flowers on the kitchen windowsill, and noticed her response on my phone.

Kelly: Tkx for invite. Shelly and I've been brainstorming. Mind if I call you now?

I didn't text but called instead. "Hey, Kelly, I'm so glad y'all have been talking about sharing the same space in the building. That's great."

"We just spoke once about it but needed your opinion. I'd love to join the conversation when you meet with Shelly. What time?"

"Five minutes ago." I laughed. "We can FaceTime when I get to the studio. See you there!"

"Bye. Bye."

* * *

I entered the studio and placed the water bottles on the floor. "It's so good to see you both."

Shelly pointed at three folding chairs. "Come sit down, Rae. I thought we might need something to sit on other than the floor." She giggled.

"I didn't even think of that. Thank you! Y'all take a water. We might need it since there's no A/C in here."

Hannah grinned and patted the floor. "I'll just sit here." She pulled a water bottle next to her.

"Well, ladies, I'm glad we're here. I talked to Kelly, and she wants to join us. She said y'all have spoken a little about sharing the same building. That's fabulous."

Shelly opened her water bottle, "I'm so glad we can include her. We knew there might not be a time when we could all be together in person this week."

I made the FaceTime call to Kelly. "Good to see this worked out."

Kelly beamed as she looked at her laptop. "I've come prepared, y'all."

Shelly removed sketches from her trendy bag as Hannah pulled toe shoes from her backpack. "Kelly, mind sharing what we talked about the other day?"

"Not at all. You know we wouldn't decide without your approval, Miss Rae."

"I want your inputs so let me know your ideas." I took a sip of water.

Kelly typed on her computer. "Instead of sharing the building space, we thought maybe we could split the building in two parts. We are thankful there's more square footage in this building than the art studio, so it just might work."

I sat my drink on the floor. "That's a great idea."

Kelly beamed. "Miss Shelly, you have the plans, I'm turning it over to you now, please."

Shelly pulled sketches from her lavender case. "Rae, the design we came up with for dance is this. We'll need a wall of full-length mirrors and two ballet barres. One should be lower than the other, so every age can learn. Good flooring is needed." She slipped into her ballet slippers, pushed out of her chair, and did a few plies' and stretches.

I watched as Shelly balanced with perfection even without a ballet barre. "You are so graceful. I must admit I'm a little envious."

"Rae, after the babies arrive, you should come for classes. The stretching and dance will be rejuvenating. Ballet slippers aren't required," she teased.

Hannah stood on pointe. "Miss Shelly and Miss Rae, since the floor is a little rough, I won't attempt any dance moves. I'm so excited about helping here and I'll do whatever y'all decide."

Kelly interjected. "Maybe after music lessons I can join ballet classes."

"And vice versa," Shelly added. "Also, I have several new pairs of ballet shoes in different sizes I can donate to children who don't have the means to purchase them. Javier has volunteered to do anything we need on the dance side and on the music side of the building."

I gave her a hug. "That's fabulous, Shelly." Then I looked at the sketches. "Y'all are wonderful. I can't wait till classes start." I took pictures of all of Shelly's diagrams and sent them to Joe,

Quinn, and Sendy. Within a few minutes I received a thumbs up from them.

I held my phone closer to Shelly and Hannah so they could catch a better glimpse of Kelly. "Okay, Kelly, your turn."

"First of all, Kramer said he'd help, too. Several guys and gals from college are willing to pitch in. There's a school in Easley that has a piano for sale at a very reasonable price. I heard it's in great condition. Shelly, Hannah, and I talked about putting in soundproof insulation in the walls between our two areas, but we know that can be a little pricey. I have a ton of music books and a few instruments that've been refurbished. We will make it work. Everybody's excited about getting to have a local music space." She added, "And a dance space, too."

I scooched out of the chair and pointed to the wall nearest me. "This needs insulating?"

All three nodded.

"Have y'all thought about a separate entryway for classes?"

Shelly shook her head. "We didn't want to add too much stuff, Rae. We appreciate all you're doing already."

"Y'all are the best. I'll do a little checking with Dr. D and Mr. Dells to find out if its too extravagant to have two doors leading into the building."

Hannah palmed her forehead. "There's already a front door and a back door to the building. Why don't we use both for entryways?"

Kelly applauded. "You are brilliant, girl!"

I sent info about the music studio to my hubby and the rest of the crew and received a smiley face emoji from the recipients.

"Ladies, meeting adjourned!" I sniggled. "Let Dr. D and Mr. Dells know your plans have been approved!"

* * *

I left the meeting feeling at peace. These ladies knew what to do and I felt completely at ease leaving the building in their hands. *Praise the Lord!*

Praise the Lord. Praise the Lord, you his
servants; praise the name of the Lord.
Psalms 113:1

Chapter 37

Friday morning arrived. Joe dragged the decorated box off the front porch and inside the foyer. I sent a text to the Historical Society Ladies, requesting they sort the names and narrow it down to three choices. We'd send out the three selections and request people vote via e-mail.

Grace called. "Rae, I'll get the girls together this evening. You can't be involved since you're one of the owners of the recreation area. Lottie will send you a text with the three choices after we adjourn, and she finishes the minutes for the meeting. Have a good evening. Bye."

I never said a word. I started to mumble something under my breath that I'd later regret, but I bit my tongue. Thankfully.

* * *

Sendy's plane from Texas landed on time and the cottage was ready and waiting. I slipped into my VW Bug and drove to Buds and Blooms. I must admit, I dreaded the thought of working with Pearl Chandler until I parked and noticed Emily at the entrance to the flower shop. I shoved out of the car seat and up to the store doorway.

"Emily, what are you up to, Girl? You look adorable."

"Well, Rae, I wanted to brighten the day before Mrs. Chandler got here. I have a smock for you to wear, too. Come inside."

"Where did you get these aprons? The multi-colored polka dots look so cute." I slipped my new uniform over my head.

"I made them last night. I know I'm taking a risk, but I made one for Pearl Chandler, too. I hope she likes it."

Within seconds the bell jingled above the flower shop door. Mrs. Chandler stood in the miniscule entrance as Mr. Chandler laughed. "This sure is a small place. How are y'all going to fit in here?"

Mrs. Chandler glared at him. "We'll fit just like we're doing now. You can leave now, Mr. Chandler. I'll call when the work is done."

A chill ran down my spine when her voice grated at sweet Mr. Chandler.

Emily didn't hesitate and slid between Pearl and her husband. "Here, sir, I'll open the door for you." He left the shop, then Emily pivoted toward Pearl and gave her a smock. "Hope you like this, Mrs. Chandler. We girls are a team now."

Mrs. C stood in silence. "I can't fit into that contraption."

Emily placed her hand on the counter. "Oh yes, you can. I called Martha last night and she gave me your dimensions."

Pearl rolled her eyes and attempted to get the polka dot smock over her head. I scooched close enough to give her a helping hand. No words were exchanged.

Emily sat on a stool near the counter. "Mrs. Chandler, we've heard you're a Master Gardener. Rae and I need all the help we can get."

"Who told you that?" She drummed her fingers on the counter. "Never mind. Guess it doesn't matter. Now let's get to work, team members." She smiled.

I'd never ever seen her smile and almost went into shock. "Mrs. Chandler, please instruct us. You're the professional."

Emily adjusted her smock and climbed off the seat.

"Call me Pearl." She straightened her gray bouffant hairdo. "I printed a list of today's orders off the website. We have ten arrangements for this afternoon." She pointed to the refrigerated containers. "We'll finish at least half of them before lunch, take a thirty-minute break, then get back to work." She held her breath as she squeezed between the counter and the shelf with vases. "Girls, these are the ones to use. Fran was very specific in her directions."

The Pearl Chandler flower shop day went without a hitch. I could even say it was actually a little fun.

* * *

Grace and Lance arrived home Sunday. The society ladies made sure their fridge was filled with fresh fruit and frozen meals. Emily and I had made a flower arrangement for them and placed it on the entryway table.

On Monday morning, my mom-in-law sent an e-mail to everyone in town:

Fran will be home this afternoon. She's doing as well as possible and wants me to thank y'all for helping. She won't be needing anymore assistance at this time and hopes to be back to work in a couple days. Also, the meeting I'd scheduled online for this evening about July 4th is cancelled. The society ladies got everything done while I was away.

* * *

Joe and I delivered mini bags of macarons and individual thermoses of milk to the bungalows. We tapped on each door, so the occupants knew they had a goodie on their porch swing.

After returning to our domain, we munched on items from a small charcuterie board my hubby had prepared for a light supper. I sank into our comfy sectional, popped a purple grape into my mouth, and almost fell asleep. Until I received a text.

Grace: Hopeful in Hope; The Gathering at Hope; Belonging in Hope

Me: Thank you

Time for bed. Time for rest. Time for sweet dreams.

When I smiled at them, they scarcely believed it... Job 29:24

Chapter 38

Days skipped by and Fran returned to Buds and Blooms. Pearl Chandler stayed on to help with arrangements for as long as Fran wanted or needed her. Our dear friend knew we all stood ready if she or her family needed anything at all.

July 4th weekend arrived in all its red, white, and blue glory. Grade schoolers and their families had lined the Beaufort Street sidewalk with small flags, and the high school band practiced for one last time before the Hope parade the next day.

A string of guests lined up in the foyer to get keys to their cottages. Since four were already occupied, three were ready to be filled.

Joe stood near his antique desk. "Ladies and gentlemen, welcome to the Inn at Hope. We're glad you're here. It'll be a fun Independence Day weekend." He waved to his cousin at the back of the line.

I strolled to where he and his family stood. "Marcus and Patrice, it's so good to see y'all. Baby Bella, I can't believe you're already six months. You're precious."

Patrice patted my shoulder, "Rae, you look fabulous." She bounced Bella on her hip. "Wanna hold her?"

I reached for the baby and held her close. "Thanks, Patrice, I needed that boost, even if you're only kidding." I pointed to the dining room. "Let's grab a seat."

Patrice sat next to me, "I'm not joking. Are you getting the nursery ready?"

"Not yet. Joe and I might have to move out of the Inn."

"Why?" She glared.

"The home Joe's folks live in is assigned to whoever runs the university here in Hope. Since Joe took the job, we are next in line. Problem is, I don't want to move."

"That must have been a shock for you and Joe."

"It was. Joe's folks were surprised, too. We're all going to talk with the main campus personnel to find out if that rule can be changed."

"Hope you find out something while we're here."

"Me, too."

Marcus trudged our way with his backpack on and the baby carrier in one hand. "Family cottage is ready and waiting." He grinned.

I handed Bella to Patrice. "You know we're only a text away if y'all need anything."

Patrice cradled her daughter on her hip. "Same goes for you, Rae."

* * *

Everyone settled into their cottages, so Joe and I had time to ourselves in our upstairs domain.

"Rae, what are you thinking about?"

"How did you know I'm thinking about something?"

"Two parallel lines between your eyebrows."

I swatted at him. "I'm concerned about moving to your folk's house. I love the life we have at the Inn."

"I know, but let's not jump to conclusions." He patted the sofa cushion. "Come sit down, Mrs. Byer. It's going to work out like it should. The one positive is the house is bigger with two bedrooms downstairs. That might be easier with babies." He shrugged his shoulders when he noticed me glaring at him.

"Joseph, change the subject."

* * *

173

Joe and I strolled to Molly's Restaurant for supper. My dear friend and chef extraordinaire, Molly, sat next to Grace at a full table of family and friends. We meandered in their direction.

Joe walked to his mom and dad's chairs and hugged their necks. "It's good to have y'all back in town."

I waved to them. "Good to have you home."

Molly pushed out her chair. "Come here, Rae. You need to sit down."

I shook my head. "No ma'am. You sit." I glanced around the room. "Where's Henry?"

"He's in the kitchen with Sidney."

I sashayed across the room, went behind the counter, and into the kitchen. "Henry, please sit and dine with Molly. I know she needs time with you. Just point me in the right direction and I can help." I tapped my foot on the tile floor.

Sidney giggled. "You need to listen, Daddy. Mrs. Rae means business. You know I have everything under control." She handed me an apron and a hair clip, then returned to the orders she was filling.

Henry didn't hesitate. He took off his apron, straightened his collar, and pushed open the swinging door into the dining room.

"Put me to work, Sidney." I held a spatula in my hand when the swinging door opened and in walked Emily.

She placed her hands on her bump. "I'm here to help, too. We pregnant women need to stick together."

Sidney twirled around. "Hey, I don't fit into that category, ladies! And I don't want to!"

Emily stuttered. "Well...well, I didn't mean you. Sorry, Sidney."

The three of us moved in tandem with Sidney at the helm. "Rae, Emily, please take those to table four."

I glanced over my shoulder at our fearless leader. "How do I know which table is which."

"There's a number on the table."

"I've never noticed."

We delivered comfort food to customers, then returned to the kitchen and made several deliveries with only a few mishaps along the way. After serving, we removed our aprons and snuggled into a booth next to our hubbies. Sidney delivered the turkey and dressing special to the four of us. Our hubbies had delayed eating until we were with them. *Sweet men.*

* * *

We got home, let the dogs out, then in, and I padded to the kitchen freezer. "Want some dessert, Professor?"

He trailed after me, reached around my waist, and kissed me. More than once. "That's all I need." Crooked grin.

"Hmm, maybe you'd better kiss me again. I can't decide whether ice cream is needed or just your smooches." I tilted my head up for another.

The knock on the back door startled both of us and set the dogs into a frenzy. Joe shrugged, then went to check it. "Come on in, Quinn. Looks like it's starting to rain."

"Ah, it's nothing. I've been stranded on a horse at the ranch when we've had storms. Now Sendy, on the other hand, didn't want to chance jumping puddles to come over here." He walked into the mud room, grabbed a dog towel out of the hamper, and dried his crew cut.

I cringed. "Uncle Q, that's a dirty doggy towel."

"Doesn't bother me." He dried his face then threw it back into the hamper.

Joe led the way. "Let's sit in the kitchen on the stools. Can I get you something to drink? Coffee, hot tea?"

"Nope. I have limited time. Sendy and I are having popcorn and a movie at the cottage in thirty minutes." He scratched his head then drummed his fingers on the counter. "The grand opening for the splash pad thing and corral is Sunday, the 4th. If it rains all night and tomorrow, I'm not chancing my horses getting hurt in the mud."

Joe folded his arms. "You're the horseman. You call the shots, Quinn."

Uncle Q clomped to the back door. "I'm going to check on the horses at Val's stalls. Wanna come?"

Joe looked at me. "Mind?"

"Not at all, as long as I don't have to." I opened the freezer drawer and pulled out a pint of pralines and cream. "I guess this dessert will have to do." I winked at my hubby and got a spoon. "Uncle Quinn, don't forget you and Sendy have movie night in twenty minutes." I kissed Joe and moseyed upstairs with the mongrels close behind me.

* * *

Joe got home and came upstairs with a pint of mint chocolate chip ice cream. "That didn't take long, did it, Beautiful?"

"I can't believe y'all got back so quickly."

"We wouldn't have, but Sendy called to remind Q about the movie. She has him trained."

"Hmmm, maybe I should take a few pointers from her." I patted the cushion on the couch. "Just kidding. I like you just the way you are."

He snuggled on the sofa next to me. "Remember how we thought it was weird that the Inn is on Charleston Street when it's not a street?"

"Uh-huh."

"Charleston Street used to be the road to the dorms and buildings. Uncle Quinn plowed a path from here to the land when we rode in his truck. It can be an official road again when more construction is done."

"That's great news!"

We reclined on the sectional with a cozy mystery on the television. The four dogs stretched on the floor beside us and snored in unison until we all went to bed. *Good night, Lord.*

*This service that you perform is not only
supplying the needs of the Lord's people but is*

*also overflowing in many expressions of thanks
to God. 2 Corinthians 9:12*

Chapter 39

Sunday morning sunrise. Joe and the dogs were nowhere in sight. I sat on the side of the bed, stretched, and took a sip of water from the glass on the nightstand. My phone lit up with a text from the professor.

Joe: At land with the dogs. No mud anywhere. Quinn brought two horses to corral. Earnest and his team got here early too.

Me: When did you get there?

Joe: Five a.m.

Me: Thanks for not waking me. I'll get dressed and ready for church. Are you coming?

Joe: Be home in 30 minutes. Makeshift sign is hung at the entryway to the land. Everything's under control.

Me: Smiley face emoji

I checked my e-mail and noticed a message from Grace to the entire Historical Society: Ladies. Don't forget today is July 4th. Set up is at 1:00 at the land. George has all the sparklers we need for tonight. Paddle boats are ready. Be there or be square.

I sent back a thumbs up emoji.

* * *

Molly and Kelly worked in the kitchen and had preparations down to a science. I hugged their waists and snatched a piece of crispy bacon from a platter. "Ladies, you've outdone yourselves. This bacon is the best." I crunched.

Kelly giggled. "You say that every time we cook, Mrs. Rae. But I don't mind hearing it again."

Molly added fluffy pancakes to the warming dish. "You bless us, Rae, and you don't even know it." She winked, pushed the door open into the dining room, and placed the pancake-filled dish and bacon platter on the French sideboard.

I followed behind her with a tray of sweet butter, syrup, and honey, then halted in my tracks when I entered the dining room. "Molly. This looks so beautiful! The red tablecloths and small flags in the center of each table are breathtaking. I'm so glad you used white and blue cloth napkins." I placed the items next to the pancakes. "Thank you. I know our guests will love it."

The back screen door slapped shut and in walked Sendy. "You're right. Guests will love it!" She quick stepped to Molly. "I've been praying about your surgery tomorrow, sweet friend. It seems we've known each other forever."

Molly laughed. "We have since kindergarten!" She slid her arm around Sendy's waist. "Mind helping me in the kitchen?"

Sendy saluted her, "I'm at your service!"

As the dining room filled to the brim, I enjoyed chatting with the guests as all nestled comfortably into their chairs. Mrs. Chandler waved as she and her husband sipped coffee at a table for two. I sashayed their way. "Good to see y'all this morning."

Mr. C smiled. "Rae, you and your staff have outdone yourselves."

Mrs. C patted his hand. "Let the girl get back to work, Mr. Chandler." She set her cup on the matching saucer. "If you ever need a side job, you're quite the flower arranger." She grinned.

I stood in amazement. "Thank you, Mrs. Chandler and Mr. Chandler." I did an about face and traipsed back into the kitchen. *I can't believe the change in Mrs. Chandler.*

Molly, Sendy, Kelly, and I stirred, mixed, and prepared additional items for the buffet. I stopped before entering the dining area. "Kelly, I hate to put you on the spot. Would you sing something to the guests?"

She didn't hesitate. "I'd love to." She removed her apron and pushed open the swinging door into the dining room.

We stood in the kitchen and listened to Kelly sing a cappella. The patriotic songs gave us goosebumps. Upon hearing bravo and applause from the cottage dwellers, we entered the room. Molly hugged her daughter tightly then turned toward Sendy and me. "Group hug, girls." We cradled in her embrace. Then she added, "Now, let's finish here and get ready to celebrate our country's Independence Day. I can't wait to ride a paddle boat and wave sparklers in the air!"

* * *

I went upstairs, changed into a red dress, then added ruby red lip gloss. My phone buzzed.

Lauren. "I know you're getting ready for church. Just wanted to catch you before the celebration this afternoon. How are things going?"

"It's good to hear your voice." I sighed. "The corral is finished and so is the splash pad. The restroom building is finished, too." I chuckled.

"That's great. But how are you doing?"

"I'll be better after sweet Molly has her surgery tomorrow. I hope all goes well."

"Rae, how is Molly doing now?"

"She worked in the kitchen this morning with her daughter, Sendy, and me. We all laughed when she told us she planned on riding in a paddle boat and waving sparklers in the air."

Lauren cleared her throat. "Then you know what, dear sister? Molly's chosen to be joyful and celebrate. I believe she'd want y'all to do the same. Enjoy today and tonight."

"You are so wise, Sis."

Lauren chuckled. "Well, I'd better go. I know church is soon in your time zone. Love you!"

"Wait a sec. What are you and Mick doing to celebrate?"

"We're going to a Milk Can dinner on another rancher's land this afternoon. Then several folks are coming for fireworks on Grandma Alana's ranch near the pond."

"That sounds fantabulous. Those fireworks will be competing with the starlit sky. Beautiful! Love you!"

"Love ya, too. Bye, bye."

* * *

Joe and I scooted next to his folks in the sanctuary pew. No words exchanged. Just a fleeting glance from Grace and a grin from ear to ear from my dad-in-love.

The choir sang a medley of patriotic songs, and the pastor kept us all engaged as he preached from Philippians. The sermon ended with a reminder about the festivities at the lake.

Grace tapped me on the shoulder as we exited the pew. "Rae, don't forget to bring potato salad and bug repellent. I've already reminded the rest of the ladies in the society." She shoved past me and peered over her shoulder in my direction. "By the way, Lauren is in for a big surprise when she gets back to Hope."

Lance patted my shoulder and whispered. "Potato salad and bug repellent sound like a lousy combination to me." He winked. "See you in a while."

* * *

Emily and I dawdled along with potato salad in hand and bug spray in our cloth bags. Our hubbies followed close behind. We all halted at the entryway to the recreation area as Uncle Q and Sendy moseyed in our direction. The Hope-ites crowded into the area.

Mayor Sounds held a megaphone to his mouth. "Ladies and Gentlemen. Thank you for participating in choosing the name of our new recreation area." He motioned for Nathaniel to stand by. "Drum roll, please." The high school drum team rat-a-tat-tatted in unison. "Today we unveil the name of our recreation area. Tug the rope fellas!" The words, The Gathering at Hope, gently blew in the breeze as we all cheered.

Victoria waved enthusiastically in our direction, then pointed at the long tables under a weeping willow. Joe and Blake detoured toward the corral.

Grace strutted toward Emily and me. "I know y'all are excited about the name, but we must hurry up, girls. We start serving in fifteen minutes." She snatched the bowl from Emily and carefully maneuvered my yellow bowl from my arms. "The masses are arriving, and we Historical Society ladies need to put our best foot forward."

Emily giggled. "Mother, I can't hop on just one foot. I'm putting my best feet forward."

Grace ignored the comment and practically sprinted to the tables.

I discreetly gave my sis-in-love a thumbs up. "Wanna detour and join the boys?"

"I wish."

The two of us knew that wasn't happening. We'd never hear the end of it, so we joined the rest of the hysterical ladies and others at the tables. My dad-in-love, Lauren's daddy, and Mayor Sounds manned the grills, while Kramer, Kelly, and their friends guarded and taste-tested the desserts at four long tables.

Some time elapsed and Mayor Sounds blurted into his megaphone, "It's time to celebrate our Independence Day, ladies, and gentlemen. Pastor, mind blessing this meal?" He didn't wait for an answer and handed the preacher the mcgaphone.

"Lord, thank You for this gathering of family and friends. Thank You for creating this great land. Amen."

A line formed on both sides of the tables as everyone filled their plates with Southern comfort food.

Joe's eyes widened at the mound of macaroni pie I'd piled in the center of my plate. "Save some for me, please."

I set my plate on the buffet table and lightly punched his arm. "Remember, buster, I'm eating for the babies, too." I added a piece of fried chicken, a dabble of cream corn, and fried okra, then proceeded to a table near Emily and Collette.

The professor set his plate next to mine, slid next to me on the picnic table bench, and whispered in my ear. "Best wife and best babies in the world."

I leaned in closer to him and kissed his cheek. "Wanna bite of okra?"

He scrunched his nose and shook his head. "Never!"

Earnest, Collette, and Daisy sat across from us. Collette bounced Daisy on her knee and attempted to take a bite of potato salad. Baby Daisy whimpered, squirmed, and chewed her pudgy fist.

Earnest reached for his daughter. "Collie, let me take her. You eat while I walk with Daisy. Hey, Joe, that might help your baby fall asleep, too."

Collette grinned. "Sweet man, they're having more than one baby at a time. They'll both be walking." She fluttered her lashes at him and took a bite of the creamy potato salad.

Joe bit into his juicy chicken, then wiped his chin. "Thanks for the advice, Earnest. I need all the help I can get."

Baby Daisy burst into tears as her daddy walked back and forth nearby. Collette pushed off the bench. "I'll take her, Honey. You can't give her what she needs right now." She smiled.

"Excuse me, y'all. I'll be over there." She pointed to a chair under a cluster of trees.

I knew this would be one of the last meals I'd share for a while with Collette since Earnest's job was complete and they'd head back to Beaufort. "Mind if I join you?"

"I'd love it."

Two are better than one, because they have a good return for their labor... Ecclesiastes 4:9

Chapter 40

Dusk arrived and Joe clipped leashes on Puffs, Buddy, and the two gargantuan pups. We strolled to the lake for the paddle boat/sparkler event. I pulled a red wagon filled with blankets as my hubby navigated our four dogs toward our beloved bench.

Emily and Blake sat nearby on their trendy folding chaise lounges. Roxie's little beagle ears perked when she saw our canines. She didn't make a peep, but wagged that miniscule tail of hers, then circled a couple times and laid on Blake's lap. Sweet pup.

The church youth had a popcorn fundraiser popup booth near the paddle boat dock. Joe and Blake took the dogs and made a beeline for the snack tent while Emily and I relaxed. Until her mother, aka my mom-in-law, stood in front of us.

Grace tapped Em on her noggin. "Girl, aren't you going on the paddle boat? We need to support the youth."

Emily darted out of her lounge chair like a bullet. A feat not many pregnant women could imitate. "Mother, I'm not riding on that contraption. Blakey and I have a box of sparklers we're sharing with everybody who's landlocked." She patted her baby bump. "After all, you wouldn't want me falling into the lake, would you?" She poked out her bottom lip and did the best pouting I'd ever witnessed.

Grace's eyes goggled. "Well, I swanny dear. Of course I don't want you and the baby to fall in the water. I just remember when you were a girl and loved those boats." She hugged her daughter and patted her tummy. "Let me know if you need anything, Sugar."

She glanced in my direction. "You, too, Rae."

The stars twinkled and the sparkler-laden grounds around the lake lit up like a gazillion fireflies. Every paddle boat on the lake carried four people and multiple sparklers. It was radiantly radiant. Breathtaking. This Independence Day was my best ever. My hubby, our precious pups, our extended family and friends, and my baby-filled tummy. Nothing better.

* * *

That night, our bed nestled us and rose and settled ever so slightly with each doggy snore. Joe slept soundly as I attempted to count sheep. *Good night, Lord. Please be with sweet Molly.*

*Rejoice always, pray continually, give thanks in
all circumstances... 1 Thessalonians 5:16-18*

Chapter 41

Before dawn, Joe hung a note on the door handle of each cottage reminding dwellers that a continental breakfast would be available. A little later, Natalie and her crew arrived and delivered pastries and fresh fruit to the Inn's dining room for our guests. Flowered paper plates, paper cups, and plastic utensils sat at one end of the sideboard so everyone could serve themselves. Fresh coffee brewed in the kitchen and a large carafe of juice chilled in an ice bucket.

* * *

All the Historical Society ladies climbed into the church bus. Church members filled the remaining seats. We were on our way to the hospital in Greenville to supply moral support for Henry and his daughters as they waited for Molly's surgery.

Emily and I shared a bus seat and watched as Grace stood at the front of the vehicle and counted heads. My sister-in-love looked in my direction and rolled her eyes. "You'd think we were preschoolers. I'll be surprised if Mother didn't bring a rope for all of us to hold on to, so we don't get lost at the hospital." She pulled an apple from her bag and crunched it. "Want one?"

"Ha-ha. I'm good. Thanks, though." My phone rang and I snatched it from my backpack. "Lauren, everything okay?"

"It is. I wanted to let everyone know we're praying for Molly even way out here in Wyoming. Please keep me posted, Sis. By the way, I absolutely love the name, The Gathering at Hope. Love ya."

"Love ya, too."

Grace remained standing and pulled a bullhorn from her leather bag. Just as she held it to her lips, my dad-in-love, the bus driver, reminded her, "Wife of mine, please stay seated. Plus, honey, you don't need that contraption."

My mom-in-law shoved the megaphone into her bag, turned and plopped into her front seat. "Well, I swanny, Lance. I wanted to lead everyone in prayer."

Her husband cleared his throat. "Well, I swanny, Grace. The Lord hears our prayers even when we whisper. No bullhorn needed."

No one made a peep until Lottie reached over the back of Grace's seat and tapped her on the shoulder. "Please pray."

Lance kept driving as the rest of us bowed in prayer for our dear friend, Molly.

* * *

The waiting room filled. We gathered around Henry and the girls as Pastor David led us in prayer. "Dear Lord, Thank You for loving us and for creating Mrs. Molly. Please bring her through this surgery and her recovery, Lord. Please keep her family strong as they wait. Your will be done. Amen."

Emily squirmed in the waiting room seat and Grace paced back and forth. Although Molly's surgery was on a different floor than the ICU where Joe's dad had been with his Pulmonary Embolism, it still brought back that memory.

My dad-in-love pulled a chair in front of Emily so she could put up her feet. I watched that tender moment of a daddy's love for his girl. I missed that feeling. I missed my daddy.

Within a few minutes, Lance came my way. He pulled a chair in front of me like he did for Emily. "Rae, put your feet up, girl. Can I get you something?"

I teared up and gulped. "You've given me what I need most, Dad. Thank you."

He cocked his head and started to comment when Grace took his hand and led him where other seasoned Society ladies and their spouses sat in a group with Henry.

If he only knew how thankful I was.

* * *

Natalie and Shelly delivered muffins and coffee. They served everyone waiting to hear about Molly's surgery, as well as those on the edge of their seats waiting for another loved one's results.

The hours seemed to drag as we waited. We stopped talking when Molly's doctor entered the room and motioned to Henry.

Henry and his daughters stepped into a nearby glassed-in room with the doctor. We could see Kelly and Sidney hugging each other and then Henry pulling them into his embrace. Within a short time, the doctor returned to the surgical unit and Molly's sweet family came into the waiting room.

We sat in silent anticipation until Henry said, "Thank you, Jesus."

The pastor asked if anyone would like to join us in prayer. We formed a circle in the waiting area to pray for those still in surgery. Such a touching time. Such a witness to others.

* * *

As the bus shuttled us back to the church, I sent a text to Joe and one to Lauren to give them the news about Molly. Lottie informed us that another plan was in effect and that she had set up a website to sign up for meals for Molly's family.

Before we got back to the church, Grace swung around in the front seat. "Hey, y'all. Don't forget to pick up your trash before you leave."

Victoria cupped her hands around her mouth and sarcastically blurted to her friend, "Yes, Mother! Bless your heart."

Grace shook her head, fluffed her hair, and added. "Lance and I are going to Gill's for lunch. Y'all are welcome to join us."

She attempted to smirk at Victoria. "Yes, I'm inviting you, too." She got up from her seat and quick stepped to Victoria and hugged her neck. "We're a force to be reckoned with, aren't we, dear friend?"

Victoria giggled. "We sure are."

* * *

I declined the invite to Gill's and drove back to the Inn. I needed to check on guests since I'd been gone since early morning. A small moving truck idled in front of the Inn.

I parked next to it, slid out of my Bug, then stepped onto the porch, and into the foyer. Joe zigzagged around his desk in my direction. "Hey, Beautiful. Did ya see the truck out front?"

I folded my arms. "Couldn't miss it. Is someone moving?"

"Not exactly."

"Then why is the moving truck here?" I flopped into the chair. "Don't be so mysterious, Professor."

"Go to cottage four, please." He folded his arms and walked to the front doors.

"Why? Do the Chandlers need something?" I shook my head and mumbled. "Is the moving van bringing some of their stuff here? Are they staying in the cottage even longer?"

He smiled that crooked grin of his, palmed his forehead, and opened the doors. "Follow me, Mrs. Rae Byer."

I reluctantly slid out of the chair and followed his lead. The two of us strolled to cottage four. I would have fast-walked past him, but I didn't have the stamina.

"Joe, I don't want to disturb the Chandlers."

The front door to the cottage opened abruptly and out jumped Lauren. "Surprise, Mrs. Byer!"

I fumbled over my words and hugged my sister's waist. "What-what are you doing here? I thought you weren't coming for a few weeks!"

She gave me an extra squeeze. "Change of plans." She motioned for Joe and me to enter the cottage. "Y'all have a seat."

I glanced around the room. "Wait a minute. What happened to the Chandlers and where's their stuff?"

Joe grinned from ear to ear. "We wanted to surprise you, Beautiful, and it looks like we did. Chandlers were even in on the whole thing. They left last night while we were at the celebration and will rent the home they're purchasing until the final paperwork is done." Crooked grin. "Mick drove that truck here with a few things from his grandma's place. Plus, he delivered Lauren early."

I glared at my hubby. "Joseph William Byer, I can't believe you kept that from me. I'm always so good at reading you."

He took both my hands in his. "Remember when you told me you were pregnant, and I already knew? You didn't read me then." He laughed.

"Guess you're right." I pretended to mope for a second then turned to Lauren. "Dear sister of mine, I talked to you on the phone earlier and let you know about Molly."

Lauren giggled then sat on the bed. "I didn't want you to know we were heading this way. I'm not going back to Wyoming until October when the university has a long weekend. Mick and I decided to slow down on the bed and breakfast renovation."

Parallel lines formed between my brows. "Will the B&B stay empty?"

"Nope. Grandma Alana made sure she had plenty of funds saved for the property. There's no need to rush into changing things till Sendy's son and daughter-in-law live in the place for several months."

I felt my brows ease a tad.

Lauren took a deep breath. "We asked them to make a list of ideas they believe would make it easier to run the bed and breakfast. Plus, we have your suggestions. Candace and Caleb are helping us, and we're helping them because they can live there rent free."

I blubbered and stumbled over my words. "I-I can't believe it!" I hugged my dear, dear friend. "I just can't believe it!"

Lauren and I started to jump up and down, till I realized my baby belly hindered my feet from lifting off the ground.

Joe opened the cottage door. "I'm going outside to help Mick. He's taking the truck to a storage unit." He looked at me. "I thought you'd like this."

"I love it."

* * *

Lauren and Mick settled into cottage four, then later that evening we all strolled to Molly's Restaurant to help Sidney and Kelly with the special meal for the evening. There was no need for Henry to close the restaurant while Molly healed. There were enough of us in town capable of helping so they wouldn't lose business.

* * *

Joe snored softly and I laid wide awake. I couldn't help myself and gently nudged his shoulder.

He jolted upright. "Rae, are you okay?" He rubbed his eyes and stared at me.

"I was just thinking about the Chandlers. God worked it out, didn't He?"

He flopped back on his pillow, cradled me in his arms, and whispered. "Yes, He did."

It was a night of rejoicing that our dear friend's surgery went well, a night of friends reuniting, and a night of family we'd chosen.

Thank You, Lord.

Finally, all of you, be like-minded, be
sympathetic, love one another, be
compassionate and humble. 1 Peter 3:8

Chapter 42

Waking up to the scent of apple pie delighted my senses. I slipped into a pink seersucker dress, Dutch braided my hair, and puttered downstairs to the kitchen.

"Kelly, it smells delicious in here."

She pulled a pie from the oven and swiveled in my direction. "I hope I didn't wake you."

"No, you didn't, but the cinnamon-y fragrance did!"

"Mrs. Rae, I know we don't need to feed anybody today because family is staying in the two cottages, but I thought I'd experiment with a new recipe." She welled up and tears streamed down her cheeks.

I didn't say a word but instead bundled her into my arms.

She caught her breath. "Do you have a minute?"

I tore a paper towel off the roll. "Here you go. And, yes, I have more than a minute."

We perched on the island stools. I handed her a fork, cradled mine, then pulled the pie closer to us. "Kelly let's be the taste testers and enjoy this for breakfast. Dig in and please share what's on your mind." We clinked our forks together in cheers-like fashion.

As I was about to take my first bite of the sensational flakey crust and fruit filled delight, my phone buzzed. I silenced it.

"Mrs. Rae. I'm letting my parents down." She bit into a piece of pie. "They want me to work at the restaurant when I graduate from college." Her shoulders drooped. "Kramer will graduate vet school next year and we have plans."

A quiver ran down my spine. *I don't know what to say.* I reached for another bite.

Kelly inhaled. "We want to get married when we graduate. Kramer's Aunt Val offered him a position at her hospital when he finishes vet school, and I want to teach music at the elementary school. Guess I could serenade the animals he'll take care of until I'm hired. I also love creating new recipes." She jumped off the stool. "Want some milk?"

"I'd love some. You have so many great talents to choose from." I snatched a couple napkins from the basket on the island.

Kelly filled our glasses then sat straight as an arrow. "Oh, I still want to teach music at the new music studio. I'd love to give back to the community."

"That's great." *Please don't let her ask my opinion, Lord.*

Kelly took a gulp of milk. "Please pray for me. I'm scared to tell my mom and dad. Now that Mom has had this operation, she might not want to be on her feet all the time at the restaurant." She took another drink. "Do you think my mom will still want to work?"

I reached for her hand. "Kelly, I can't answer for your sweet mother. It sounds like you have a lot on your mind, and I'll bet she has some time to listen. Why don't you take the rest of this pie to her. See where God leads the conversation."

"I'll clean up the mess." She glared at the mixing bowls and utensils in the sink.

"No, you won't. I will. You have more important things to do, Miss Kelly. Now, skedaddle." I hugged her neck.

"Thank you for helping. You'll be a terrific mom."

I wrapped the pie in cellophane and handed it to her. "Enjoy, sweet girl." I opened the back door and the two of us stepped outside. "By the way, I loved your new recipe."

Kelly waved as she opened the backyard gate and headed for home.

Thank You, Jesus.

When anxiety was great within me, your
consolation brought me joy. Psalms 94:19

Chapter 43

The days skipped into August. Two weeks till school would start. Almost the end of summer.

I made a last-minute call. "Good morning, Lauren."

"Hey, Sis. How are you?"

"Didn't know if you had time to go to breakfast today. Maybe have a girl's day?"

"Penelope and I are walking to Bitty's Buns. She's helping Natalie at the bakery." She twittered.

"That's fabulous." I added. "You're already having a girl's day with Penny."

"Just for a few more minutes. She'll be with Natalie till lunch. Why don't we meet at Fenster Haus in thirty minutes if that works for you."

"Perfect. See you there. Tell Penny I said hi!"

"Wait a minute. Someone wants to talk to you."

"Mrs. Rae, it's Penelope."

"So good to talk to you."

"My puppy, Rosebud, is such a good dog and I'm taking special care of her. Papa told me Rosebud can sleep with me now. She goes potty outside and won't wet my bed." She giggled. "Bye, Mrs. Rae."

"Goodbye, precious."

* * *

Puffs, Buddy, and Trixie sprawled on the living room rug. "Are you missing Heidi? She needed to go home with Lauren and Mick." They lifted their humongous heads off the floor for a few seconds. "You're the best listeners ever." I gawked at my reflection in the mirror. *I can't believe I'm only five months pregnant. I'm huge.*

The dogs ran down the stairs in front of me and scampered into the kitchen. "Y'all slow down. I can't keep up." The scent of homemade waffles filled the air. "Molly, it's so good to have you back."

"I missed being here." She used tongs to remove the waffle and murmured. "I'm so glad you talked to Kelly."

"I really didn't say much to her."

"Oh, yes you did. She said you told her to talk to Henry and me. We're so glad she followed through with your advice. As you know, she doesn't want to work at the restaurant after she graduates from college. We never knew." Molly layered the fresh waffle on top of two others. "We came up with a plan, but I need to run it by you first."

"I'm all ears." I attempted to wiggle my ears to no avail.

"Kelly would love to work here part time till she graduates. Maybe take over for me on holidays? I told her I'd mention it to you."

"I love that idea. Then she can test new recipes." I poured more batter into the waffle iron for Molly. "I'm saying yes to the idea."

She laid the tongs on the counter and wrapped her arms around me. "Thank you, Rae." She stepped back. "Well, I swanny, dear. Those babies are certainly growing."

"You can say that again." I snickered.

* * *

Lauren and I sat at a table near the back of the windowed restaurant. Shelly gave us our menus. "So good to see you two here together. A while back, I mentioned I had something to tell you about Mick's grandparents and mine."

Lauren patted the chair next to her. "Please tell me. I'm all ears."

I said the same thing earlier, sister.

Shelly took the menus. "Let me take your orders first."

We ordered our usual and settled comfortably into the cushiony chairs while Shelly quick stepped our way and sat next to Lauren.

Shelly grinned. "Just letting y'all know there's no mystery involved in what I'm about to say. I might have led you all down that path. I'm glad we finally get to talk."

Lauren smiled. "I did a little investigating on my own while I was in Wyoming."

I sat across from the two of them and hung on their every word.

Shelly giggled. "Then you know."

I couldn't help myself. "Know what? I'm in limbo here!" I sniggled.

Lauren laughed. "You tell her, Shelly."

"When my Granny and Pop came to America, they didn't know where to live. They went to a nearby train station, gave the teller at the ticket booth every penny they could spare, and asked how far it would take them." She filled her glass with water and took a sip. "They were given one-way tickets to Cheyenne, Wyoming. Mick's grandma Alana and his grandpa had reservations on the same train. They noticed Granny and Pop sharing a piece of bread." She took another sip of water. "Mick's grandparents bought them a warm meal and the four of them visited. Before they arrived in Cheyenne, Mick's grandma and grandpa took a gamble and hired my grandparents on the spot. They remained friends till they passed."

I leaned in on my elbows. "That's a great story!"

Lauren wagged her finger at me, "Oh, no, Sis. That's not the end of it."

Shelly gave a toothy smile. "Family settled in that area. Mick's great aunt and my great uncle grew up together and married. We only found out Mick and I were cousins when Alana

Griddle passed away. We never would have known if records hadn't been found in all the paperwork your hubby went through." She gently elbowed Lauren.

I shook my head, "Did I get this straight? You and Mick are cousins so that makes you and Lauren cousins by marriage?"

They said in unison, "Yes!"

The time spent explaining it all over again, made everything a little clearer. Family. The very best.

An uncle or a cousin or any blood relative in
their clan may redeem them. Or if they prosper,
they may redeem themselves. Leviticus 25:49

Chapter 44

Joe and I woke up early for my five and a half month OB/GYN appointment in Greenville. I felt a little winded. Joe tied my trendy tennis shoes for me and we paused every couple of steps as we crept downstairs.

Molly greeted us in the kitchen, "Well I swanny, dear. You look a little peaked. Let me get you some cool water and a wet paper towel for your forehead."

I willingly waited for her pampering. "Thanks, Molly. I do feel parched."

She handed me the water and gently patted my forehead with the cold towel. "That should help, dear. It's hot as blazes today and those two babies are giving you extra warmth. You and Joe should go to lunch after your appointment. That's just a little motherly advice."

Joe nodded, put ice in a plastic bag, and snatched a small cooler from the mud room. "Let's take this with us, Beautiful." He looked at his phone. "Better run."

I held his hand. "I'd rather walk."

"Oh sure, Honey. I'll move slowly."

"Joseph William Byer! Have you lost your sense of humor? I was only joking!"

Crooked grin. "As you can tell, I'm not really in a joking mood. I'm worried about you."

I squeezed his hand and motioned for him to tilt his head toward mine. "I know, and I love you for it."

Molly scampered ahead of us and opened the front doors. "Take your time. We'll be praying."

* * *

We cruised down Beaufort Street in our VW Bug and passed Bitty's Buns. I noticed Lauren and Penny sitting outside at one of the iron tables under the striped umbrella. Within seconds a text came from my dear friend/sister.

Lauren: I'm praying for your appt

Me: Thanks, Sis

Lauren: Molly let me know how you're feeling. Everyone knows.

Me: How does everyone know?

Lauren: She told Grace after me and the rest is history.

Me: Exclamation points!

* * *

The doctor viewed my ultrasound, then placed the stethoscope in her ears, and listened to the babies' heartbeats. "Well, well--"

Joe stuttered. "What, what does that mean?"

I lay as still as possible.

"You already know you're having twins."

Joe mumbled. "Yes."

The doctor swung the stethoscope around her neck. "Better get ready for triplets. Evidently that little one hid behind the other two."

Joe placed his hand on my belly. "Three?" He plopped into a chair.

I felt myself tense. Then I bawled.

The doctor patted my hand. "I'll give you both some time to process this news." She removed her gloves and added, "All three babies look healthy and that is a praise."

Joe dragged himself out of the chair. "Rae, Honey, we're in this together."

"No, we're not. You're not carrying three babies, I am." I turned my face away from him. I couldn't catch my breath.

Joe handed me a tissue.

I blew my nose and whimpered. "I don't know what to do."

He held my hand until the doctor returned. "Dr. Farr, does Rae need to do anything differently now?"

I blew my nose again.

"I know this is a shock for y'all. Sometimes a baby isn't visible in the beginning."

I sat up as straight as a pregnant lady carrying triplets could do. "You mean there might be another baby?"

"No, Rae. Three babies. You'll need to do what you're doing now. We'll monitor you closely. There is a possibility they'll deliver early. We knew that could happen even with twins." She handed Joe and me a tissue. "You both are a team and will get through this. I know it's easy for me to say because I'm not pregnant."

I nodded.

"I usually don't share this with others, but I'm telling you." She pulled up a metal swivel stool. "I have three boys. Born at the same time." She grinned.

Joe wiped his eyes. "You mean, triplets?"

"Yes, I do."

I gulped. "Dr. Farr how did you manage?"

"Just like the two of you will do. My husband and I have faith and rely on family and friends."

"We do have a lot of support." I whispered.

Dr. Farr got up and pushed the swivel chair near the wall. "When others offer help and you need it, take them up on it. When folks offer help and you don't need it, be honest and tell them." She washed her hands in the sink. "Set up boundaries early. I have a few websites you might enjoy that focus on parenting triplets. The receptionist will give them to you. I'll see you in a couple weeks."

Joe wiped his brow. "Thank you, Dr. Farr."

She smiled at the two of us. "Take time for each other. A strong marriage is the best gift you can give your children." She exited the room, and we followed close behind.

* * *

I slid onto the passenger seat of my VW. "Joseph, I'm scared. Are you?"

He closed my door, trotted to his side of the Bug, and folded himself inside. "I'm scared to death." He leaned in and kissed my cheek. "Rae Long Byer. Three babies."

I felt puddles forming in my eyes.

"We're in this together like we've always been." He grinned that crooked grin of his.

"I'm numb about the whole thing."

He started the engine and turned on the air conditioner full blast. "Want something to eat?"

I rubbed my belly. "We definitely need sustenance. How about a burger and fries."

"I thought you'd like something fancier like Sweet Pea's Southern Bistro. We loved that place."

"That's a great idea. The doctor told us to take time for each other and that'll be perfect."

Our red Bug puttered into downtown Greenville. Joe found a spot close to the bistro and we meandered to the entryway as if we'd been there a gazillion times.

The hostess led us to a table nestled in the corner of the room near the window.

Joe excused himself. "I'll be back in a sec, Beautiful."

I sipped my water and unfolded my napkin. As I perused the menu, a major battle between meatloaf and pasta ensued. I craved both.

Within minutes, my hubby returned. "Rae, these are just a small symbol of my love for you. Four yellow roses symbolizing our babies and one for you."

"Aww you sweet husband." I gently took them and enjoyed their vintage scent. "Where in the world did you find these?"

"I saw a flower cart before we came inside." He settled into his chair and looked at the menu.

I smelled the roses, then heard a familiar laugh. "Joe, that sounded like Lauren." My eyes canvassed the area.

Lauren peeked around the corner. "Hey, Sis."

Mick strolled hand in hand with her toward our table. "We saw y'all when you came in but didn't want to bother you."

I wiggled out of my chair and clung to Lauren. "You're not bothering us."

Lauren gently hugged me. "Rae, you're shivering. Everything all right?"

"Uh-huh. Wanna join us?"

"Yes, dear sister."

The server set two extra chairs at the table and handed Mick and Lauren menus.

Joe eased back in his chair. "I can't believe y'all came here, too. This was a last-minute choice for Rae and me."

Mick raked his fingers through his thick waves. "Lauren said y'all liked this place, we had some time, and thought we'd give it a try." He leaned toward Lauren and planted a kiss on her cheek.

Lauren reciprocated then looked my way. "How'd everything go at the doctor today?"

Joe interjected. "Let's order first, because we've a story to tell."

We gave the server our orders, then Lauren drummed her fingers on her glass of sweet tea. "Okay, y'all. We placed our orders, now spill the beans." She pretended to scowl. "Please." She took a sip.

"Sis, you, and Mick are the first to know. I'd have called you when I got home, but this is even better." I shifted in my chair. "Well Auntie and Uncle, there are three babies in this belly of mine."

"Triplets? I can't believe you're having triplets!" Lauren jumped out of her chair and almost tripped over the chair leg. "We'll have a baby shower. I can't wait! No wonder you're bigger than..." She stopped mid-sentence.

I snickered. "Go ahead and say it." I chuckled.

Joe added. "Bigger than she thought you should be."

Mick shook Joe's hand. "Good job, Joe."

Lauren and I looked at the two of them and said in unison. "Men."

We chatted over meatloaf, pappardelle pasta, seafood, and assorted sides. The waiter served us family style because we were family.

* * *

Joe didn't drive to the Inn. Instead, he parked in front of Peaches and Cream. "How about a cone? We can take it to our bench."

I nodded. "Buffalo Chips for me, please. Two scoops." I didn't budge.

He practically skipped around the front of the Bug and opened my car door. "I know you're staying in the car, but I needed to kiss you. You're my sugary sweet dessert."

My eyeballs rolled. "Professor, that was over the top. I repeat, way over the top. Now get me some ice cream." I folded my arms across my ample middle and sniggled.

* * *

Joe exited the ice cream shop, and I scooched out of the car. He handed me both cones then pulled an old sheet off the back seat. "Want to carry this and I'll carry those." He pointed his chin at the ice cream.

"I'm good. Better hurry, though, cuz you might not have any ice cream left. It's melting. I'll help you out." I licked a drip off the side of his waffle cone.

We strolled to our bench near the lake.

He tossed the sheet across the bench. "Come sit down, Mrs. Byer." He took his cone.

I squinched as close to him as I could then flipped off my shoes. "Ahh, the grass between my toes feels wonderful." I took several licks of the creamy delight, then finished the first scoop of ice cream before it had a chance to barrel to the ground. "Whew! That was close!"

Joe put his arm on the back of the bench. "This is our proposal bench, our baby reveal bench, and now our family bench." He nuzzled my neck.

"You romantic man. This is our bench." I patted the sheet. "Nobody elses."

We munched and crunched our waffle cones and reveled in this moment. Until a tap on Joe's shoulder startled us.

Joe's mother scampered in front of us. "Appointment today. How did it go?" She pushed up her three-quarter sleeves. "I took Emily to her doctor visit today. It was scheduled right after yours. She's doing just fine. Are you?" She pulled a tissue from her pocket and patted the back of her neck.

Joe stretched and stood beside her. "Mother. All is well." He grinned and waved. "Hey, Dad."

Grace's pursed lips melted into a frown. "That man's crimping my style."

Lance snuggled next to her. "What in the world are you doing, Sugar? Come on, let's head to Greenville for dinner. I heard about a new place."

Grace side-stepped. "You're not going to schmooze me, Mister. I'm just checking on my grandbabies. Emily is good. Now we need the latest on Joe and Rae's."

He reached and held her close. "Boundaries, dear. Boundaries. Remember how we loved that when we were young?" He raised his brows. "Now let them be. We've got dinner waiting."

Joe shook hands with his dad. "Where are y'all going?"

My dad-in-love announced, "Sweet Pea's Southern Bistro."

Joe and I didn't say a word.

Grace and Lance's hands threaded together as if one. As they sauntered toward Beaufort Street, Grace swiveled in our direction. "By the way, we got an e-mail about the house we're living in. Looks like y'all might have to move there within a year. Whether you want to or not." She turned.

Lance yelled over his shoulder, "It'll all work out, Youngsters!"

Joe bellowed. "We'll need all the space we can get.".

We both laughed uncontrollably.

Grace halted in her tracks. "What's so funny, Son?"

"That's the second-best news we've heard all day."

She scuttled in our direction, pulling Lance behind her. "What's the first?"

Joe and I slid over on the bench. "Have a seat you two."

Grace muttered. "Just tell us".

Lance sat. "Gracey, please sit down."

She slipped next to him.

Joe held my hand and cleared his throat. "Mother, thanks for letting us know about the house. It might come in handy."

Lance and Grace sat on the edge of the bench. Neither uttered a word.

Joe nodded at me. "Want to say something, Honey?"

"The appointment went well. A little unexpected."

Lance reached for my arm. "What's happening, daughter-in-love?"

Joe held up his three fingers and I copied him. "Mom and Dad. On the count of three listen."

Grace and Lance shrugged.

Joe announced. "One, two." He pointed at me, and we both yelled, "Three!" Three babies. We're having triplets!"

Grace's jaw practically fell on the ground and Lance shoved off the bench. He grabbed Joe in a bear hug. "Son, you did good. I can't believe it!" He shuffled toward me, bent down, and hugged my neck. "Little Lady, you did extra good. I'm gonna have triplet grandbabies!"

Grace fluttered. "Triplets!" She stood and stared at my bulging middle. "No wonder you're so big!"

Joe started to comment, and I touched his hand. "No need, Hubby. She's right." *I'll give Grace some grace.*

Joe and his parents plopped down on the bench. We spoke over each other with enthusiasm until we heard cheers and barks. Emily and Lauren held onto Puffs', Buddy's, and Trixie's leashes then released the hounds. Our fur babies romped our way and sat on the ground near our feet. We heard other family and friends belting out a chant. The only words we deciphered were, "Rae and Joe, one baby, oh no! Three it'll be."

The rhyme wasn't the best ever written, but the words were the best we'd ever heard.

This is our family bench, Lord. Thank You.

More to Come